T0116993

THE WATCH DOG IS MAD

(3rd in the Bachelor Preacher Mystery Series)

Bob Wyatt

authorHOUSE®

AuthorHouse™
1663 Liberty Drive
Bloomington, IN 47403
www.authorhouse.com
Phone: 1-800-839-8640

First published by AuthorHouse 5/10/2011

ISBN: 978-1-4567-5050-3 (sc)
ISBN: 978-1-4567-5049-7 (e)

Library of Congress Control Number: 2011907411

Printed in the United States of America

CHAPTER ONE

A few weeks ago, I watched a pair of birds building a nest. The two birds flew around and inspected limb after limb until they found just the right location. I marveled at how they took twigs, mud and candy wrappers to mold and shape their home on a branch. It wasn't long before I spotted the first speckled egg in the nest. It was an exciting day for me as I considered the prospect of having a family of birds outside my window.

A half dozen times I chased the neighbor's cat from the tree as she attempted to grab the little eggs. The mother bird saw my efforts and we became friends as she sat on the eggs keeping them warm. She knew I respected her but her male counterpart was a different story. He was noisy and worked to keep me well away from the nest. The father bird flew around wildly flapping his wings, diving at me and chirping loud warnings to stay away.

Then came the special day when the eggs began to hatch. It was awe inspiring to witness the birth of three baby birds. It was one of God's natural wonders taking place. Such a wonderful act! Yet, the cute adorable little birds immediately demonstrated their healthy lungs by beginning to make loud chirping noises.

Since then, by 6 a.m. every morning the tiny birds begin their blaring screaming songs suspending any possibility of further sleep. I find myself responding by springing into an upright sitting position each morning with my hands tightly clasp over my ears. The shrill shrieks that continue result in a reaction in me akin to sticking a finger in an electrical socket or turning the television volume to its highest level and then turning on the power. The birds at full throttle warble away with high pitches that cause my ears to throb, my teeth to grind, my hands to crush the pillow around my head in an attempt to regain the peaceful silence of the room before being disturbed.

Remarkably, this morning was different. The song sounded optimistic. It wasn't panicked or shrill. The birds' musical chorus was almost melodious giving the feeling that all was right with the world. The sound was calling me to get out of bed and tackle life. I felt this strange impulse that something good was going to happen if the rapidly growing birds were singing a pretty song.

The rising sun hit my face as I continued lying in bed contemplating this surprise. I rolled over placing my back to the window. The sun's warmth made me pull my legs to my chest as I curled up to get more sleep---yet the persistent sound of the birds' singing set me to thinking---wondering what special surprises would occur and who I would meet during the new day? I pulled my pillow closer and enjoyed how it felt to lay there in the sun listening to the pleasant song of the birds for a change.

Reflected in the mirror I could see the mother flying on the branch with some food for the little birds. She was a good mother. She provided the babies with all their needs. I smiled at the beauty of the love and caring that existed in the bird family.

Warming up quickly from the sun I used my foot to raise the window a bit and immediately felt a gentle breeze against my body. I drew my foot back under the cover. The scent of the honeysuckle growing on the trellis next to my front door was intoxicating as it drifted in the open window. It added to my desire to roll over and sleep a little longer, but the finale chorus of the birds' chirping began. I knew it was time to get up.

Suddenly, the clock-radio clicked on and the loud announcer gave the weather broadcast. He reported "clear skies all week!" I lifted up and looked out the window just in time to spot Dollie Burgess, my landlord, walking a fast pace with the neighbor's cat.

There was not one excuse I could bring to mind to keep me in bed or from going to work.

"It can't get much more beautiful than this day," I thought to myself. "I need to do something special. I need to call on extra people or maybe buy some Danish from Porter's Place and distribute them to various elderly members of the congregation. Yes, I like that idea. That would be sort of like the mother bird providing for her flock like a preacher should provide for his congregation."

I'm Rev. Jack Temple, the bachelor preacher at the local Nickerson Street Church here in Sassafras Springs, Missouri. Although I have only been here a few years, I've found the community to be a warm and caring one. Each day brings surprises and revelations about the various people in the congregation, but they are all wonders to behold as they live out their lives.

One thing that became very clear the first month was that everyone has a mystery in his or her life. I don't mean some deep dark secret, although a few of those exist, but each member has something he or she is battling. Everyone has a challenge that keeps his or her life on edge.

As you see the people around you day by day you would think they are mostly a happy people with nothing to give them stress. They all have a joke or story to share with their friends and neighbors. They all seem secure in their positions.

Take Josh McDaniel, editor of the local newspaper, for example. He doesn't attend the Nickerson Street Church but has become a close friend to many members of the congregation including myself. He provides encouraging words and assistance to all of us who are around him.

Josh supported the fundraising efforts when money was raised to replace the church's roof after a tornado passed dangerously close to the building last spring. He was there when the choir needed robes for the community choir competition. In recent weeks he provided stories in the local newspaper about the congregation's effort to provide a youth center for the community.

He is a great example of what the members should be like. I'm confident he will become a member when the time is right.

Beyond the façade lies a number of interesting mysteries in Josh's life---some he knows about and others will be revealed in time. That's the way it is with most of us.

My hope is that he will start attending services and become an active member. From my observations and my experiences, God works in mysterious ways and I'm confident in time a good man like Josh will find the church.

For this story, Josh isn't the main character. Rather it is an intern that worked for Josh at the local newspaper during last summer. Lee Downs was his name. He was a trim athletic looking city kid with his name brand clothes, perfectly styled and trimmed hair, and a moustache. He was a natural flirt, oozed with compliments for those around him, and spoke with a slight New York accent.

Lee immediately became a part of the Nickerson Street Church and a faithful member of the choir, but his story brought a lot to the "front page" before his mystery was revealed.

"Hi, Jack," said Josh McDaniel as he entered Porter's Place for a cup of early morning coffee and a pastry. "What is that smell? I haven't smelled anything that wonderful since my grandmother quit making homemade rolls when I was 16."

"Good morning, Josh," greeted Rev. Temple. "What's the news in Sassafras Springs? Anything new happening in town?"

Josh nodded his head negatively and sat down across from Rev. Temple.

"Welcome," interrupted Ike Winston as he poured a steaming hot cup of freshly brewed coffee and sat it in front of Josh. "What do you two have planned that has brought you here this early?"

"I'm here looking for news," replied Josh McDaniel.

"I'm on my way to a Vacation Bible School planning meeting," replied Rev. Temple.

"I know you two better than that," said Ike as he raised his eyebrows. "I bet you have something on your mind. You are always up to something."

"Not this time," laughed Rev. Jack McDaniel. "I smelled your pastries and how could anyone pass this place without stopping for something?"

"I need a story for the front page of the newspaper," said Josh McDaniel while rubbing his stomach in anticipation of the freshly made pastries Ike would soon be setting in front of them. "The deadline is noon. You have any suggestions?"

"Ike knows everything happening in town," commented Rev. Temple as he turned to look at Ike who was holding a tempting plate of long johns. "You can think of something that might be newsworthy. What do you have for him?"

"I know better than to carry tales or to share things told

to me in confidence," laughed Ike Winston with a twinkle in his eyes. "That is the secret to knowing things. You don't share them."

"But then what fun is being aware of lots of things if you can't share them with someone?" responded Josh McDaniel.

The two men nodded in agreement as each of them took a long john from the plate and began to eat. Immediately groans could be heard from them as they tasted the flavors of the pudding and the pastry. Rolling their eyes and moving their free hand to their waist they unconsciously examined their waist lines and took another bite.

"We have a special on chocolate éclairs. Two for the price of one today. Is that newsworthy?" asked Ike Winston.

"Not sure that is headline news because you always have the best pastries in town at a good price," laughed Josh McDaniel. "Would you box a dozen of those éclairs? I'll take them to the newspaper office. Maybe that will inspire my workers to bring in the news."

"Ike, you do have a good sense about you on what to share and what not to share with others," began Rev. Temple. "I remember when a group of the board members from the church happened to be here. You were here too but didn't spread news about the meeting until the group had a chance to meet at the church building to officially adopt the plans."

Ike Winston nodded, "I suspected sharing that information would have stirred up a debate and your congregation has needed that kitchen for a long time. You didn't need me looking big by knowing something I wasn't supposed to know."

"It was a month ago," continued Rev. Temple as he turned his head to face Josh McDaniel. "We happened to be here by coincidence. Steve Elsea commented he had been in the church kitchen and the cabinet door fell off right after he found he couldn't open one of the drawers. The men started talking and the whole discussion evolved into the need to replace the cabinets and to expand the kitchen into the classroom next door to provide more space. The same men met for their monthly board meeting at the church and made the plans official a week later. Ike kept quiet about it until it was officially voted on at the church. I personally appreciated that."

Porter's Place had become a regular place for meeting in the community thanks to a warm and friendly proprietor and great food. The farmers felt welcome enough to gather for a morning cup of coffee where they would complain about the weather and the politicians and spread gossip about who was selling what. Most mornings the economy would be a prime target.

Many a city council decision was discussed and planned while enjoying Ike's hospitality. It was right in that same booth that Josh McDaniel had decided to accept the call to be president of the local Lion's Club and Rev. Temple had felt called to be the minister of the Nickerson Street Church. The quiet friendly atmosphere in the old building was perfect for most to settle down and prepare to meet the problems of the day or to sort thru the challenges of tomorrow.

The former bank building was located at the main corner of the business district downtown. It was one of the first buildings built when the town was founded in 1895. The town had definitely seen a better day in the business district with many of the buildings empty, but there was still a unique and quaint visual of the wonderful past when looking at the store fronts.

Porter Conway had worked at the Bank of Sassafras Springs an incredible eighty years including serving as president the final forty. Every customer at the bank knew they would be greeted first by Mr. Conway when they walked in the bank and he would bid them farewell as they left. He had left quite a record when he died at age 100 a year earlier. His shadow was everywhere in the old building and the new bank owners new it. They wanted to make their own statement and finally decided to abandon the building for a new one---"signifying a new beginning." The Bank of Sassafras Springs built a new facility a few blocks from the original one and moved the business to its new location right before the tornado in Cornelia destroyed Ike Winston's restaurant and home.

Ike and his wife were determined to remain in the area and to continue their business. They had grown to like the people and thoroughly enjoyed hearing about the history of the area from the older citizens who regularly stopped by the restaurant.

The couple looked for another building in Cornelia, but most of the business buildings had been destroyed or damaged extensively. The clean up was expected to take months from their viewpoint. Needing to get their business open as quickly as possible the couple finally decided to look elsewhere for a place to live and have their restaurant.

Nearby Sassafras Springs had its share of historical stories which is what had attracted the Winston's to Cornelia twenty years earlier. When the couple visited Cornelia the first time, the older men and women shared stories about how their ancestors fought to save the town in 1864 when the bushwhackers attacked. The evil men rode the country torching houses and shooting up cities with no concern for the welfare of the people. It was no different when the violent men came to Cornelia.

The citizens shared how their ancestors had tried their best to save the little town but finally watched it go up in smoke in a couple of hours in 1864. Nearly 200 people lived in the city limits of Cornelia at the time. The bushwackers destroyed all the houses, the school, the entire business district, two churches and the post office.

The Winston's felt these stories should be preserved and had provided photographs and a write up of the history in their place of business. People enjoyed reading the information and brought neighbors and friends from long distances to see the restaurant. It quickly became a popular place.

Another story included in the displays was about how the name of the town was selected. The little village had been named by the local doctor in the 1850's who had a daughter Cornelia. Unfortunately he also had a flock of Shanghai Chickens. The attractive and unique birds had huge feather headdresses that caught the attention of the population. The doctor placed the chickens in a pin next to the road and the passersby often stopped to watch the fancy fowls. In no time at all the people referred to the town as "Shanghai: The town with the funny chickens."

The tornado destroyed about everything that had been left from those early days. With regret, Ike and his wife decided to look in nearby communities and thus it was they came to Sassafras Springs and spotted the "for sale" sign set in the window of the former bank building.

The weekend before the couple had driven around the streets of Sassafras Springs and examined a couple of possibilities, but both agreed the rundown buildings would take more money to repair than they had available. The couple nearly ended their search when Ike on his own decided to drive around one more time. When he walked into the former bank building he immediately visualized their future restaurant.

Sassafras Springs had a unique downtown. It was filled

with brick buildings each having their own character and a different style or color of brick. One building at the top of its front had spelled in the brickwork "Opera House - 1906" and another an American flag made out of different colored bricks to display the flag properly. According to the older citizens, all of the buildings had been built when old John T. Sassafras moved his general store from nearby Monett Station in 1895. The railroad track was under construction and John wanted his general store right next to the track to inspire the development of a new town.

Ike fell in love with the old bank building's architecture. Inside he felt the warmth and could imagine Porter Conway sitting in a chair at the front door watching all the people as they came to eat.

Ike heard his own footsteps on the wooden floors and again got nostalgic thinking about the early city fathers coming together that first winter and proclaiming the need for a bank. He imagined the early men and women debating the issues. Ike knew the story of how they had determined that first year to have a bank. In no time at all it was established and opened for business. By the end of the following year the early city fathers were building houses and businesses for the new community of Sassafras Springs.

Ike looked thru the teller windows and ran his hand along the edge of the fine workmanship of the woodwork around the doorways and windows. He envisioned the north wall and east wall with booths and a row of tables down the middle. It was just the right size for the eating area. The space behind the teller windows provided a great display area to have foods in refrigerators with see thru doors or glass cases to hold an assortment of pastries, pies and cakes. In the back was an area for cooking.

Checking the upstairs he envisioned living quarters. He

knew it would be tight for them financially as they rebuilt their restaurant. Having a place to live in the same building would help tremendously. The whole situation appeared perfect in his mind.

A few minutes later Ike escorted his wife to their truck where he opened the door and helped her in. She looked at him with a surprised look and began asking questions, but Ike remained quietly smiling and going about the matter of driving to the mysterious destination with his wife. As they got out of the truck Ike winked at his wife and remained silent.

When she walked in the building she immediately fell in love with the decorative metal ceiling and natural wood floors. A few minutes later they were on the phone talking to the realtor and another month later opened for business.

The couple converted the teller windows into areas for customers to order their coffee and treats. Placing stools around the counters made it have the appearance of the original bank but provided a functional facility for the restaurant. By doing this the establishment felt right at home as it still had the original appearance.

Along the walls were comfortable booths that survived the tornado in Cornelia. Ike had moved them to the new spot the first week after taking over the building. On the east wall were large windows allowing a lot of light into the building and a great view of downtown Sassafras Springs.

On the north wall, thanks to the local historical society, there were numerous pictures of Sassafras Springs from the early 1900's before cars were a normal sight on the streets. In these pictures were wagons, a bandstand in the middle of the street, boardwalks along the sides of the street, and a pump in the intersection to get water for the horses. The entire place was a fascinating sight that was soon the pride of Sassafras Springs.

The back room had to be completely rewired to provide the plug-ins and strong enough power for the many appliances they needed. Construction also included cabinets and storage units and a living area for the couple in the upstairs, but miraculously they opened in one month.

On opening day nearly every person that dropped by called the business Porter's Place. Not having thought of what to call the new business, the couple quickly recognized the value of maintaining the historic aspect of the building and accepted the name in honor of Porter Conway.

"Get me a box of those éclairs too," said Rev. Temple as he reached into his pocket to get his wallet. "The group at the VBS planning meeting would enjoy a treat and maybe that will get us in the 'work together' mode."

"Having a little trouble with people working together," chuckled Ike Winston.

"Too many leaders and not enough workers," replied Rev. Temple. "But don't get me wrong. They are all wonderful people, but sometimes they get over zealous to have things the way they think is best rather than sharing in the planning."

"Aha," responded Josh McDaniel.

"So, what is the news you have already for today's paper?" asked Rev. Temple.

"You'll have to wait for the newspaper for that one," replied Josh McDaniel. "I don't want to spoil the edition for you. But I still need a meaningful article for the front page."

"There is a birthday party north of the church on Grand Street," began Ike Winston. "I heard they were having a clown and from the appearance of the beautiful patio and yard it should be something special."

Josh McDaniel grew up in Sassafras Springs but was moved to California after his parents died. It was tough for him to lose both his parents, but thankfully he had loving grandparents who were able to take him. He had always wanted to return to Sassafras Springs and occasionally the grandparents would spend a few days in the summer visiting friends with him brought along for the ride. He loved it in the small community and made plans to return permanently after he had his degree in journalism.

When Benson VanBurg, editor of the local newspaper, announced he was retiring Josh was quick to contact him. VanBurg considered shutting the newspaper down, but Josh knew that would hurt the town. Josh couldn't resist moving back to his original home when the opportunity came to purchase the newspaper.

The community welcomed him back to Sassafras Springs. The businesses in particular knew keeping the small town newspaper in operation was essential to their success. They had watched the troubles in the neighboring town of Polenskyville when they lost their newspaper. Nearly 2/3rds of the businesses folded that first year. The school failed to pass an urgent bond to finance the school and rumors were circulating that the school would close and be annexed by adjoining districts in another year.

Josh McDaniel was a tall man in his late 40's now. He had been successful working for the newspapers in both St. Louis and Chicago as a reporter and was eager to try his hand at being editor of a small town newspaper. This was his first editor's job and sometimes he thought he might have taken on too big a challenge. Never the less, he loved the small town of Sassafras Springs and was eager to make it work.

There was a noise at the door and everyone turned to see who it was. There stood a good looking young man in his early 20's dressed in dress pants, white shirt and a tie.

His hair was trimmed neatly and he had a notebook with pen in hand.

"Jack," began Josh McDaniel as he motioned for the stranger to join them at the booth. "I would like you to meet my new assistant, Lee Downs. He comes from the Missouri University in Columbia's School of Journalism and will be working with me this summer as an intern. Lee, this is Rev. Temple from the Nickerson Street Church."

"Pleased to meet you, Sir," greeted Lee Downs.

"Nice to meet you Lee," responded Rev. Jack Temple as he stood up and shook Lee's hand. "Hope you will visit our Nickerson Street Church soon. Do you sing? We have a wonderful choir and are always looking for new singers."

"Yes, I do sing," replied Lee. "Just how did you know?"

"That deep voice had to be a good singing voice," laughed Rev. Temple. "How low can you go?"

"Not sure. Depends on the day," Lee said with a laugh.

"Well, let me welcome you to Sassafras Springs," continued Rev. Temple. "I am sure you will enjoy living here. The people are fair minded, optimistic and full of community spirit."

"I have already seen that," Lee Downs said. "When I was moving in my neighbor brought a delicious German chocolate cake. I believe her name was Dollie."

"Yes, that would be Dollie," laughed Rev. Temple. "We can count on Dollie to make you feel at home and a part of the community. Bless her!"

"I agree," chimed in Josh McDaniel. "I could use one of her chocolate chip cookies now."

"What!" said Ike Winston as he sat a coffee cup for Lee Downs.

"Dollie," defended Rev. Temple as he rubbed his stomach

to demonstrate his love for Ike's pastries. "Yours are delicious too or we wouldn't be here. But you know Dollie and her neighborliness. Lee here already has had a cake from our Dollie."

"That Dollie," replied Ike Winston. "What a lady!"

"This is Lee Downs," introduced Josh McDaniel. "Lee will be working with me this summer as an intern."

Lee Downs got up from his seat and shook Ike's hand with a smile. He observed the list of available pastries and requested the oatmeal raisin cookies with a cup of coffee.

"So Lee," began Rev. Temple as he changed the subject. "What do you plan to do to make this local newspaper more exciting and interesting?"

"I have some ideas and hope Mr. McDaniel will let me do some of them before the summer is over," replied Lee Downs looking like he was ready to take over the challenge of running the entire newspaper. Confidence radiated from every word and action.

"Yes," said Josh McDaniel, "I think I have a winner here. The professors said he was top of his class and would go far. They said he could make a story out of nothing better than anyone they knew."

"Not a lot going on in town that is newsworthy so that may be a good person to have on your staff," laughed Ike Winston as he poured more coffee for the gentlemen.

"Thank you, thank you for all these accolades. If you will excuse me I have a birthday party to cover. Are you ready, Mr. McDaniel?" asked Lee Downs.

"Well, he is a go getter," said Rev. Temple.

"I may not be able to keep up with him," laughed Josh McDaniel. "So how did you learn about the birthday party? You have connections already in town?"

The two newsmen emptied their cups and carried their pastries in napkins as they left Porter's Place. The new reporter was out to prove himself and if the phrase "early bird gets the worm" was true the town of Sassafras Springs would have a newspaper filled with news breaking stories soon.

Rev. Jack Temple sat there watching the two getting in their car outside the window and waved as the car sped off. Turning to Ike Winston he nodded he would like a coke to go and then pulled his cell phone out of his pocket to begin making some phone calls. He knew he had work to do before Vacation Bible School would be ready. It was scheduled to start in two weeks and there was still a need for two more teachers.

"I don't trust him," interrupted Margaret Cushing, owner of the clothing store next door as she came up behind Rev. Temple.

"Maggie, I was just calling you," said Rev. Temple with a surprised expression. "You don't trust who?"

"Something about that young boy bothered me," she answered pointing the direction that Josh McDaniel and Lee Downs had driven.

"Give the man a chance. He just got here," laughed Rev. Temple. "What don't you like about him?"

"Something about the way he was looking everything over," she continued. "He is trouble."

Margaret was dressed in a stylish red dress and had a white purse and shoes making a very nice appearance. She smelled delightful with a touch of perfume. Rev. Temple looked at her in an admiring way but still wondered what had caused her to not trust Lee Downs.

"He seemed too eager. Lacked the calm laid back attitude of Josh. The success Josh has enjoyed here is much in part to his understanding the people and working with us for the good of all of us. I didn't see that in Lee. All I saw was a hungry person to devour you if you looked the wrong way at him."

"My word," Rev. Temple laughed. "You got all of that in one short meeting today?"

"He bothers me. Mark my words, Jack," she warned. "We'll regret his coming to Sassafras Springs. I can feel it."

"Anyone here want a pastry?" interrupted Ike Winston. "My wife just took some fresh ones out of the oven."

Maggie and Jack both held their stomachs and rolled their eyes, but couldn't resist. They directed Ike to wrap some to take with them then picked up their coffee cups and held them mid air as they began talking about Vacation Bible School.

Maggie was the director for the two hour a night sessions that would soon start. She had asked for some help from Rev. Temple as she had some difficulties getting enough teachers for the various classes.

"With the economy the way it is," she began, "more women are working and there are less people available to teach or assist in the Vacation Bible School. Of course that is why we moved it to the night time. Still, it has been hard to get people because when the women work all day and then have to fix dinner when they get home and somewhere in their do a load of washing and try to spend some quality time with the kids they don't want to involve themselves in another job at night."

"Yes," Rev. Temple agreed, "I know it is tough to raise children any more. The expense is a lot more than when we were that age. It takes a lot of extra work these days."

"Rev. Jack, let's go over to my store and we can finish making plans," said Margaret Cushing.

They paid Ike and gathered up their coffee cups and additional pastries and exited Porter's Place just in time to see an ambulance. The sirens were blaring and lights were flashing sending shadows and red flashes all around Rev. Temple and Margaret Cushing as they stood there.

"Wonder where it is headed?" asked a concerned Rev. Temple. "Could you excuse me for a few minutes? They may need help. I have the strangest feeling."

"Go ahead," said Margaret Cushing. "If you didn't have compassion like that you shouldn't be our minister. Go on. I understand."

The minister ran to his car and pulled it into the street and headed for the sound of the siren as he worked to follow the ambulance to its destination. He quickly discovered it was not far from the restaurant. He got out of the car and ran to see who was on the stretcher being loaded into the back of the ambulance.

"Josh?" he quietly spoke. "Josh? What happened?"

Unable to get any information from the people around he looked for Lee Downs. Finally seeing the ambulance was about to leave, Rev Temple got back in his car and followed it to the hospital. Rev. Temple watched the ambulance as he quickly tried to park his own car. He could see the paramedics preparing Josh to be rolled into the hospital.

After getting his car parked he jumped out and ran to the side of the gurney. He started to ask what had happened when the paramedics pushed him out of the way and headed for the hospital double doors. Rev. Temple was filled with questions but knew he needed to remain quiet.

Once inside, Rev. Temple was close enough to see Josh McDaniel and saw the gray color of the skin and his weakened condition. There was no doubt that whatever had happened had left Josh in critical condition. He was nearly unconscious and mumbling information to Lee who wasn't to be found. The weak Josh McDaniel turned from side to side and finally seeing Rev. Temple put his hand out.

Rev. Temple was stunned seeing Josh McDaniel in this

condition when only minutes before the healthy robust Josh was joking and looking forward to a great day. Now laying helpless on the gurney he looked awful. Rev. Temple's mind rushed with questions wondering what could have happened and where was Lee Downs.

Dr. Don Boling appeared from around the corner and quickly went to work on Josh.

"Don," hollered Rev. Temple." Don, what happened?"

"Hi, Jack," responded Dr. Don Boling. "They appear to have brought Josh McDaniel in as he had a heart attack."

"A heart attack? Oh no!" Rev. Temple said as he squeezed Josh's hand.

Rev. Temple quickly got his cell phone out and started to make a phone call while the nurse led him to a waiting area. He slowly sat down in one of the chairs--his mind still racing with the news that his friend Josh was struggling to live. The phone began ringing. He took a deep breath to get some strength in his voice.

"Yes, Dollie, is that you?"

"Jack?" replied Dollie Burgess. "Is something wrong? Your voice doesn't sound right. You sound worried."

"Yes, I'm at the hospital. It is Josh. He has had a heart attack. I thought you would want to know. He is at the hospital now."

"I'll be right there."

CHAPTER TWO

Dollie Burgess and Josh McDaniel had been childhood sweethearts in the 6th Grade, but while she and her family were gone for a few years Josh moved to California to be with his grandparents. By the time she returned their romance had disappeared and both had found other people to marry. Still there was a closeness that remained and now that they were both widowed their circle of friends seemed to find ways of pairing them off more and more. Rev. Temple knew that Dollie would want to be at Josh's side.

Rev. Temple had been living in Dollie's spare room for a few months. Unfortunately lightning had struck the parsonage shortly after Rev. Temple had become minister of the local congregation. The house burned along with nearly everything he owned. Dollie Burgess quickly came to his rescue insisting that he live in her spare room. She had an outside door to the room installed making it more private for him and insisted he stay.

Dollie Burgess rapidly saw him as a "God-send" as he began repairing things around the house out of appreciation for her kindness. In the short time he had been living there he had repaired the lawn mower and taken the task of mowing. He had repaired the toaster twice, a leak under the kitchen sink, cleaned out the garbage disposal two times, and repaired the ceiling fan. Dollie's act of kindness had been returned many times over.

Dollie's son had moved to Chicago with his family the year before and she was pleased to have this "adopted son" as a part of her life now. She figured this new young single preacher would need some guidance plus some good home cooked meals from time to time. She was delighted to have Jack join her. They quickly became friends and as close as family.

"Rev. Temple," began a voice behind him. He jumped at the unexpected sound. Turning he found Chuck Stein who had lost his mother a few weeks earlier.

"Chuck! You startled me," replied Rev. Temple. "What brings you to the hospital?"

"Is it true that Josh McDaniel had a heart attack? Will he be alright?" questioned Chuck Stein.

"I don't know yet. Have not been able to find someone to give me information," Rev. Temple replied. "That is very nice of you to show such concern."

Chuck Stein looked at the ground as he sat down in the waiting room besides Rev. Temple. Rev. Temple could see Chuck Stein was very worried. His hair was fashioned in the popular spiked style though the excessive length with this style made him look pretty wild. It looked like it had not been combed for a year. His clothes, though clean, were ripped in several places with both knees sticking out. In his ear was displayed a tiny diamond stud earring.

"Are you doing alright?" Rev. Temple asked Chuck.

"Oh, yes. Just worried about Mr. McDaniel," continued Chuck. "You know, I just started work at the newspaper and I suspect this new guy that he hired will push me out if he can. We didn't hit it off very well."

"What do you mean?"

"Well, he was smarting off about how he would change the newspaper and increase sales 200% in a month. I got sort of sick of that and told him he better make sure he talked to Mr. McDaniel before he did any of those ideas of his. You should have heard him."

It was apparent to Rev. Temple that Chuck Stein was nervous about losing his job. With Josh McDaniel in the hospital undoubtedly Lee Downs would take over as editor until Josh was able to return. Rev. Temple thought back to Margaret Cushing's comments and considered the fact that Lee Downs was not to be found when he should have been with Josh here at the hospital. This news from Chuck about Lee's plans to change the newspaper made him uneasy.

Rev. Temple at the same time was attempting to reserve a decision about Lee Downs. He always tried to understand both sides of issues. He stopped for a minute to think of reasons Lee Downs was not at the hospital.

"There were regulations that prevent people from riding in the ambulance to the hospital. Maybe he was taking care of some business for Josh since he couldn't ride to the hospital," Rev. Temple thought. "If that was the case he should have been here by now or called. Then again maybe he had called. Maybe he went to the newspaper office to reassure everyone and to let them know what had happened."

"Rev. Temple," began Chuck Stein.

"What Chuck?" replied Rev. Temple as he dismissed all the questions from his mind and focused on Chuck.

"What will become of the newspaper if Josh is not able to work?" said Chuck weakly.

Rev. Temple thought for a few minutes and really didn't have an answer. Josh McDaniel didn't have any relatives that Rev. Temple knew nor did he have any connections to people in Sassafras Springs except for Dollie Burgess. He had grown up in Sassafras Springs but the population had changed tremendously since those days.

"Rev. Temple, what are you doing here?" began Joan Stacy, choir director at the Nickerson Street Church.

"Josh McDaniel has had a heart attack and I'm waiting to see how he is doing?"

"Josh! My word, what will we do without him!" she gasped. "He is constantly doing things for the community. He provides free publicity for every fundraiser, donates his time to assist in projects for groups or organizations he doesn't even belong."

"Exactly what I was thinking. Let's keep good thoughts that he will be ok. You are right though. He has been a tremendous influence in our town---all that without whining or arguing or accusing people. He somehow keeps us focused on doing good for each other. His newspaper is one of positive optimism. We benefit a lot from that."

Chuck Stein shrugged his shoulders and walked away. Rev. Temple looked at Chuck and shouted a farewell and encouraged him to come by the church office later to talk.

"Remember that story the St. Louis paper did on us and the next thing we knew the television cameras were focused on our town," continued Joan Stacy. "Josh took them aside and informed them if they were going to talk about Sassafras Springs they were going to talk about the good things. He insisted that the town didn't need to have bad things broadcast everywhere."

"True, we owe him a lot of thanks for that," noted Rev. Temple. "Our town works together on most projects because of his uniting articles. Just look around you and you can see towns that are falling apart. In their towns the editors print negative stories and constantly write divisive editorials. But not Josh. He always writes from the positive side."

The two halted their conversation as they spotted Steve Elsea entering the emergency room with a bloody towel wrapped around his hand. Rev Temple and Joan Stacy rushed to Steve's side to offer help. Before Steve could say anything the couple was pushed aside by a nurse who started asking questions while another took notes. Rev. Temple and Joan Stacy were directed to move back to the waiting area.

The two of them looked anxiously toward Steve. When the nurse started to take Steve back to a cubicle in the emergency room, Steve held his hand up signaling he wanted to say a few words to Rev. Temple and Joan Stacy. He quickly reported he had fallen at church while trying to repair the sign on the front of the church building. He had cut a gash in his arm and thought it should be examined. He was thankful the glass had not cut a major artery or vein. The nurse then led Steve to a cubicle in the emergency room.

CHAPTER THREE

"Josh McDowell sent me over to cover the birthday party for the Sassafras Springs Gazette," began Lee. "My name is Lee Downs and I'm the assistant editor of the newspaper. It is a pleasure to meet you."

Jessica Blandon looked rather startled as she had not considered the birthday party a major event in Sassafras Springs. Her little daughter of 4 years of age was having a dozen guests but she had no idea that it would be a subject for the newspaper. Now she was glad she had hired the clown and invited her neighbor, Phyllis Blakely to come and assist in the event. She did a quick check around the area and decided everything was ready to be shared with the world thru the newspaper.

There were red, white and blue streamers blowing in the wind. There was an American flag hanging above the porch swing and bunting strung around the railing. They were left from the 4th of July party she had hosted and the family reunion the previous week. It seemed appropriate to use it one more time for her daughter's birthday party. Her husband had agreed as he had been the one to climb the ladder to tack the colorful bunting to the edge of the house and was glad it was being enjoyed by several and not just the immediate family.

As Jessica Blandon thought about it she concluded that having the party written about in the newspaper would be something special to clip and put in Little Drew's scrapbook. She hoped there would be some good photographs as well.

"Come in Mr. Downs," invited Jessica Blandon.

"Please, please call me Lee," said Lee Downs as he bowed his head in a friendly fashion. "I have found this community to be a very friendly place and look forward to being here for some time. I was hired last Saturday by Josh McDaniel. He has been complaining of being tired a lot lately and said he needed someone to share the work so he sent me over. Hope you don't mind. He seems to be liked in the community and I'm sure I will learn a lot from him while here."

Jessica Blandon led Lee Downs through the kitchen where a huge birthday cake in the shape of a cartoon character was sitting. It had four large candles on it and appeared ready to be rolled on to the patio for the young birthday girl's party.

The two of them strolled out the back door and into a lovely flower garden with a brick path leading to the swimming pool. It was not a large pool. It could be described as a "kiddy" pool with the water not over a couple of feet deep. There were a dozen children trying to all be in the pool at the same time. They were splashing and having a good time.

Lee began taking pictures and interviewing the children. They were excited to think they were going to be in the newspaper. They kept asking if the report would be on television too but Lee kept informing them that he was with the Sassafras Springs Gazette and not the television. He assured them more people would see it in the newspaper this week than on the television.

Lee turned the camera toward the clown who was drinking some punch from a Styrofoam cup and trying to twist balloons to make animals. Lee walked toward him and offered to hold the cup. The clown quickly took the opportunity to free his hands and began making some very clever looking animals. The sounds of squeaky balloons could be heard followed by the screams of delighted children as they recognized the animals the clown was making with the balloons.

Lee looked around at the party. He was impressed at the thought and planning that had obviously been used to prepare such a fun event. Treats and activities were made available to the kids at just the right moments to keep them interested and having fun. The entertainment and music complimented the activities but did not get in the way of the fun for the young people. The children were allowed to enjoy doing what they wanted in groups.

At one point, a noticeable silence began to settle on the party as the young people sensed it was time for the birthday cake. Suddenly there was the sound of a fanfare coming from the house. The crash of a set of cymbals was heard as the French doors slowly opened from the dining room onto the patio. Out came Jessica Blandon rolling the fully lit birthday cake and singing "Happy Birthday." All in attendance began to applaud and sing with her. Lee quickly set the cup down and began taking pictures. He could see the headline in the next day's newspaper.

On the back of the cart with the cake was a large number of colorful balloons.

Each balloon was attached to a little bag. Inside were gifts for each child. The sight was quite festive and the children came running from all directions. Jessica handed a balloon and present to each child. They individually started ripping open the packages and shouting with joy at the surprises they had received. At the same time they were grabbing cake and eating it like sandwiches instead of using the forks provided.

Lee made a few notes on his notepad and nodded approvingly to himself that he had enough for his story. He approached Jessica Blandon with a hand extended and thanked her for allowing him to attend the party.

"This will make a nice headline for the newspaper," said Lee. "It will include pictures of your beautiful backyard and cake. You will be the talk of the town."

Jessica Blandon blushed at Lee's words. "Thank you so much for coming. My little girl will be pleased to clip the article to put in her scrapbook of this special day. You will add so much to her day with the article."

Lee Downs smiled and nodded again. He closed his notepad and placed it in his pocket and put the shutter cap on the camera as he put it inside the bag. He turned to go when Jessica Blandon caught his arm.

"Did you say headline?"

"Why, yes," answered Lee. "This is a big event here in Sassafras Springs this week. Of course it will be a headline on the front page."

"Oh, my!" she exclaimed. "Don't tell Drew. Let's surprise her!"

Lee Downs again smiled at he turned to leave. He waved to the young people who cheered for him and waved back. It had been a rather enjoyable visit and he thought he was being accepted well by the locals.

Reaching the gate to the fence around the backyard he undid the chain and opened it. As he did a large St. Bernard dog shoved the gate open and came charging in almost knocking him down. His camera bag went flying off his shoulder. In panic he jumped to catch it and was relieved to see it land in a nearby bush undamaged. He quickly grabbed the bag and turned his attention to the new scene developing at the party.

"Alright!" he exclaimed. "Now this is a story developing. Front page material. Go for it dog!"

Lee hurriedly opened the bag and pulled out the camera. He could tell this was going to be a fun moment and just what he wanted for that front page story photograph. He started clicking pictures as fast as he could.

The long haired overly excited dog ran through the crowded part of the party knocking the table legs loose on the card table set up for the cake. With a crash the table tumbled down. Cake flew everywhere sending kids screaming and running wildly to catch the dog.

The more the children ran the faster the dog lunged forward to avoid their grasps. With a running leap the dog went flying through the air landing in the swimming pool. The beautiful belly flop by the dog sent the water emptying the pool and covering everything around.

The whole scene looked like a tsunami had ripped thru the area as the dog continued to make huge splashes. The children in the pool screamed and laughed as they quickly climbed out and stood staring at the huge animal as he thrashed around.

Lee Downs moved closer clicking picture after picture of the drenched children standing in the now flattened flower bed of zinnias and snapdragons. Lee photographed the dog twisting his body flinging water every direction. The dog continued to shake his long haired coat as he climbed out of the pool making the children scream louder.

Jessica Blandon looked at the well planned party she had worked so hard to make perfect for her daughter. Here in an instant the party had gone from beautiful and organized to total chaos and it was on the verge of becoming a fiasco if she didn't get that dog under control. She lowered her head and started marching toward the dog with a determination---a focus---on getting the devilish dog.

As she started toward the dog, the dog dove back into the pool sending water flying again. Undeterred by her failure to get the dog the first time, Jessica waded in after the dog and grabbed his collar pulling it with all her might.

"Frances," Jessica Blandon firmly called as she tried to get the dog's attention. "Come here, Frances."

Jessica Blandon struggled to pull the dog out of the pool. She continued to call the dog by name. Inch by inch Jessica dragged the dog out of the pool and across the yard to the neighbor's gate.

It wasn't the first time the huge dog had paid a visit to her yard. The neighbor often walked the dog and every time Jessica Blandon's front yard would have to be carefully cleaned of the remains left behind. The neighbor and she had nearly had a war over the dog when Jessica hosted the Mary and Martha Circle's annual ice cream supper on the patio earlier in the summer. At that event she discovered that older women and that dog were not a good combination.

Every inch of the birthday party scene was being photographed by an eager Lee Downs as he clicked picture after picture. Jessica Blandon didn't notice him as she was too busy holding on to the dog collar. The huge dog tugged away and kept trying to return to the party, but a very determined mother was going to keep her daughter's birthday party a success. She strained with every ounce of strength to get the gate open to send the dog on his way home. With one final push the dog suddenly shifted gears and began running toward his own house. Jessica lost her footing and was sprawled on the lawn looking into Lee's camera. He couldn't resist taking one more picture of her bewildered look. She jumped to her feet, slammed the gate shut quickly and chained it.

"Well," she quietly said as she gathered her composure. "That's done."

Lee quickly held the camera behind his back so she would forget that he had photographed the entire event. He stood there watching as she adjusted herself to return to the party. She tossed her hair back and straightened her clothes. She pulled her apron back to the front of her body and wiped her hands on the underside of it to clean her hands and yet not soil the front part.

"You handled that rather well," laughed Lee Downs. "I congratulate you."

Jessica Blandon looked at him with a smile and continued as though nothing had happened. "Thank you again for coming. Would you like to take some cake home with you?"

"No, thank you," Lee Downs replied wiping cake off his shoes. "I believe I have plenty to take with me already."

Lee Downs nodded farewell again with a smile and a slight twinkle in the edges of his eyes as he made his way back to the car. He now had a "real" story for the front page.

"How proud Mr. McDaniel will be when he sees my first story on the front page!" he thought to himself.

CHAPTER FOUR

Back at the hospital the doctor and staff worked to get Josh McDaniel comfortable. They had oxygen tubes running to his nose. A device was connected to his chest to monitor his heart beat. An IV dripped slowly beeping as it entered his veins.

Josh had fallen unconscious but the doctor reassured Rev. Temple that it would be easier for Josh to regain strength if he was resting more completely. Being unconscious would help him to be totally relaxed rather than worrying about getting the newspaper completed or whatever else he might have on his mind.

Rev. Temple remained in the hospital waiting room to meet Dollie Burgess. When she arrived they immediately began praying for Josh to recover. A few minutes later, Dr. Boling approached them and said it was alright for them to step in the room. He reported that Josh appeared to be making good progress toward recovery, but was still unconscious.

Nurses could be seen going by the door as they paced back and forth going in the various rooms checking on the patients. Once in a while they stopped to ask Rev. Temple if he knew anything more and would take a quick glance at Josh McDaniel. Many would offer a short prayer and expressed hope that Josh would make a quick recovery. Some of them would hug Dollie and ask if she needed anything.

Rev. Temple had not realized how important Josh had become to the community. It often took a disaster or accident or illness like this to see the importance of a person. Rev. Temple decided to let Dollie have some time alone with Josh. He stepped out and went to the waiting room to sit.

"Rev. Temple, what are you doing here?" questioned Joan Massie. "Dollie isn't sick or had an accident has she?"

"No, it's Josh McDaniel."

Joan's face showed deep concern as she sat down to hear what had happened. Joan had worked as a typist at the newspaper when Josh first arrived. She later left her job when she was having a baby.

"Yes, he has had a heart attack."

"No," she said showing slight panic. "He was my boss before you moved her Rev. Temple. He was one of the nicest and most supportive people I have ever known. When I was pregnant he made sure I made an appointment to have training for being a mom. I was only 17. My parents were not supportive at all. They almost disowned me but thankfully he was there to give me encouragement and help me arrange for the birth of the baby. He didn't have to. I wasn't his family. He just did it because I worked for him and he was a good man."

"I've heard that a lot from people lately," replied Rev. Temple. "I have always liked Josh but only recently realized what a good caring person he is."

"Yes he is." she continued. "I remember the night the baby was born. I went out to get in the car and it had a flat tire. I looked around and wondered what I would do. He happened to be driving by on his way to the city council meeting to get a story for the newspaper. Surprisingly he stopped and immediately had me in his car and was rushing to the hospital. He stayed all night. He did call the city council and requested to be filled in with an article for the paper that night which they provided. He didn't have to help me. I had left my job there at the newspaper, which I might add sort of left him shorthanded. He didn't seem to worry about that. His first and foremost concern was me and my baby that night. I'll never forget him for that."

"That is remarkable," responded Rev. Temple. "I didn't think there was ever a time he would be swayed from being at a city council meeting. I'm joking of course, but he is as dedicated a reporter as any newspaper in the state has and still manages to be the editor as well. Sometimes I hear he even runs the presses himself to make enough money to keep the newspaper in town."

"That's right Rev. Temple. That newspaper isn't a money maker. He has to make most of his money from print jobs… and with the new technology of copiers and printers there isn't nearly as many of those jobs available."

A nurse motioned Rev. Temple to come to Josh McDaniel's room. Rev. Temple quickly got up and began his way to the room and then turned to Joan Massie. Rev. Temple took her hand and thanked her for her kind remarks about Josh and invited her to join him in a quick look in the room. She nodded and thanked him but said she feared she had a cold coming on and maybe she should wait a day or two. She asked Rev. Temple to be sure to let Josh know that she was praying for him.

Rev. Temple went to the door and slowly pushed it back to see Josh McDaniel. He was quite a sight with all sorts of contraptions attached to his body. Dollie Burgess was holding his hand and smiling, talking softly and praying on the window side of the bed. Rev. Temple stepped inside and she immediately got up. Rev. Temple motioned for her to sit back down.

"He is conscious again," said Dollie Burgess. "Not ready to talk much though. Said he was still feeling pain and rather scared at the whole experience."

"No surprise there," said Rev. Temple. "Having a heart attack is no small matter. Glad to see he is gaining strength. Any word from the doctor the past few minutes? He had been good to keep me informed the first few hours but hasn't said much lately."

"Afraid he was here for a few minutes but left without saying a thing," reported Dollie. "Josh, it is Rev. Jack. He is here to pray with you."

"Jack?---cough," started Josh McDaniel.

"Oh no, you don't," said Rev. Temple quickly. "You rest. I'll do the talking this time. You are my captured audience. Now let me pray for your recovery and good health."

Josh nodded approvingly and appreciatively. He closed his eyes and was quiet as Rev. Temple prayed. After the prayer Josh McDaniel turned to Dollie Burgess and pulled her away to ask a private question.

"What's wrong?" Dollie Burgess asked.

"Has Lee Downs been here?" he asked.

"Who," she asked. "I don't know anyone by that name."

"Lee Downs. You know---the one who is the summer intern at the newspaper. I met him this morning."

"First I've heard of him. You say he is a summer intern? Well, it is about time Josh got some help for that newspaper," she said as she turned with a look of relief. "He works way too many hours."

Dollie looked down at Josh and shook her head. She

thought of the many hours he must work in getting the news, typing it and then setting it up before finally printing it. She looked at him horrified that he could be in such a helpless condition at the moment.

"Lee Downs?" she questioned as she returned her thinking toward Rev. Temple. "Is that what you called him?"

"Yes, but don't you think it is strange that he hasn't been here at the hospital?" questioned Rev. Temple.

"He probably isn't in town yet. When did Josh say he would get here?" Dollie Burgess responded.

"Get here? I met him this morning with Josh at Porter's Place. The two of them were on their way to cover a birthday party when Josh had the heart attack. When I got to the ambulance, they were loading Josh in it and Lee was not to be found anywhere."

"That does seem strange, but I'll bet Josh told him to go on to the birthday party and to prepare an article for the newspaper so they could get it in the issue that comes out tomorrow."

Rev. Temple shrugged his shoulders. Of course Dollie Burgess was right. She always saw the good in a person and often would bring Rev. Temple's suspicious mind back to reality. He had often depended on her input to calm a situation down that he would have blown out of proportion. It was good to be living at Dollie's house and to have this good Christian's encouragement and advice.

"I think you are right Dollie," began Rev. Temple, "but I think I'll drive by the newspaper to see what is happening. He should know how Josh is doing and how much we all care about him."

Rev. Temple gently shook Josh's hand and gave him some encouraging words then left to drive to the newspaper. Rev. Temple hoped he would find Lee Downs there working on the newspaper but was still disturbed that Lee had not made an effort to contact the hospital about Josh. Then again, maybe he had. Maybe all this worry was a result of Margaret Cushing's warning earlier in the day.

CHAPTER FIVE

There was a lot of commotion in the front part of the newspaper office when Lee Downs entered and motioned for the two volunteer neighborhood reporters, the ad saleslady, the printer, and typist to come together for a brief meeting. Lee shared how he had seen their editor near death as the paramedics took him to the hospital. He then handed an article to the typist and stressed how he had been told by Josh to go to the birthday party so that the story would be included in tomorrow's newspaper. He reported how Josh had done everything he could to provide the information needed so that the newspaper would be ready the next day. The intern then instructed the staff to help do the job just like Josh would expect.

"People aren't going to want to know that Josh was ill and taken to the hospital if they don't get their newspaper," Lee remarked. "They are going to want their newspaper and that is what Josh wants us to do. We must work together to get the next issue on the street and in the homes on time."

The staff quickly went to work for their employer and friend Josh McDaniel. They were eager to let Josh know they could do the jobs that most of them had been trained by him to do. They would show him he had nothing to worry about. They would keep the newspaper running smoothly. They all agreed that would help Josh to relax and quickly recover.

The smell of chlorine and newsprint drifted throughout the office. On one side were filing cabinets with information on nearly every person in town. The files contained every article written about each person and some additional items from neighboring newspapers. These articles came in handy when needing information to fill out a story on an individual's accomplishments or recognitions. There were files on the various organizations, churches, businesses and government. There were drawers of past issues of the newspapers and additional drawers of information that could be used as filler for weeks when the news of Sassafras Springs was slow.

When Lee saw Rev. Temple enter the front door he quickly approached Jack with a concerned look. Rev. Temple looked around and could see things were running smoothly. There was Sherry Martin typing a stack of articles and preparing them to be clipped for laying out on the layout sheets. She stopped to wave at Rev. Temple.

He could see George Robbins in the backroom running the press with what looked like envelopes. There were six cases lined up to print. In front at her desk was Charlotte Stokes adding up lines of numbers as she worked on preparing the monthly financial report of the money she had brought in from selling advertising.

"Glad to see you have everything under control," began Rev. Temple. "I was concerned when I didn't see you at the ambulance. It seemed like you would have wanted to go to the hospital with Josh to make sure he was alright."

"I was going," responded Lee Downs, "but he wanted me to cover the story and to get the newspaper out on time. You know Mr. McDaniel better than I do, but I suspect you understand how important it is for him to get every newspaper out on time. It is sort of an unwritten rule of the press."

"Perhaps you are right," commented Rev. Temple. "He is intent on getting the news when he knows there is some out there. He will go to a meeting the night before the newspaper is released and stay up all night to insure that the information is included in the newspaper even if it means reorganizing the entire front page."

"That sounds like a good editor," replied Lee Downs.

"I have talked to him from time to time about how difficult it is to get people to submit the news," continued Rev. Temple. "Usually the same people who won't turn the news in are the first ones to criticize when something isn't included. Josh has the idea that if a person complains about the newspaper not having an article it is partially that person's fault for not telling him. You can't print what you don't know."

"Exactly," laughed Lee Downs. "That is what we need to get across to the public. Turn in the news or it may not be included."

"Josh had a catch phrase that he told me," began Rev. Temple. "He said, 'He who doesn't toot his own horn may not get it tooted.'"

Both laughed and agreed that Josh McDaniel was correct in the case of newspapers. An editor or reporter can't report what they don't know. Rev. Temple promised Lee he would be better about providing news articles or leads to the newspaper office and thanked him for working so hard to keep the newspaper going for Josh.

Rev. Temple shook Lee's hand and wished him luck running the newspaper as he left convinced that Lee was doing a good job. Rev. Temple chuckled to himself as he left the office as he remembered what Margaret Cushing had said that morning. She said he was "trouble for the community."

"How surprised she would be to see Lee smoothly running things," thought Rev. Temple as he got in his car and headed for the church building. "I better get to work on my sermons and then I'll check back at the hospital later this afternoon. It should be interesting to see how Lee puts the newspaper together."

Immediately after Rev. Temple left the office, Sherry Martin began questioning some of the articles. She stopped typing and started reading it. She looked over at Lee Downs for a second and then started typing again. Finally she halted.

"What is this article about a mother involved in arson?" asked a surprised Sherry Martin.

"Type it as I wrote it, Sherry," responded Lee Downs. "That is our lead story on the front page today."

"Arson by a mother! Right here in Sassafras Springs?" said Sherry Martin as she shook her head in disbelief. "Wow!"

"Just type it as is and get it to me as soon as you can so I can get the first page set up," Lee instructed.

"Yes Sir, Mr. Downs," replied Sherry. "I'll get right on it. You are a good editor already, Sir. Thanks for being here to take over."

That made Lee Downs smile. He had plans for the Sassafras Springs Gazette. He was going to break all sales, increase advertisement and was aiming at doubling the number of subscriptions.

Sherry Martin's fingers clattered away on the keyboard as she quickly typed the paragraphs Lee had written. Tossing her hair back she came to an abrupt halt. She looked up at Lee with a puzzled look. She shook her head and lifted the paper from the stand. Her mouth was wide open in disbelief as she turned again to Lee.

"Mr. Downs? Ah, are you sure you want to write this article this way?" questioned Sherry again.

"What is the problem now?"

"Well, this arson thing? Ah--, if I read correctly she was lighting a birthday cake. Don't you think that headline is a bit misleading?" quizzed Sherry.

"What do you think will sell more newspapers? MOTHER SETS FIRE AT HOME or Mother Lights Birthday Candles?"

"I see your point but----."

"Then type it. We are here to make money. All of your jobs depend on us making money so let's get out there and do it."

"Yes sir, Mr. Downs," said Sherry Martin with a questioned look. Shaking her head she returned to typing the article.

At the sound of a bell she looked back up from her typewriter to see someone entering the newspaper office. Lee Downs immediately ordered her back to work saying he would take care of it.

Entering the office with a manila envelope was a beautiful girl with long black hair and brown eyes. She revealed a very nice tan around the top of her sweatshirt. She was obviously in excellent physical condition and her attire signaled she had been out for a morning jog. She turned to look at Lee Downs with a smile and blink of her eyes. Lee's heart was racing.

"Good morning," greeted Lee Downs as his smile widened and eyes sparkled.

"This is the financial report released by the mayor's office. I was over there and they asked if I would drop it by," she reported.

Lee took the envelope and handed it to the secretary who thanked the young lady and said she would be sure to give it to Josh McDaniel when he returned.

"That was very nice of you. What is your name?" said Lee as he continued to study her. "I'm new here and rather eager to get to know people in town."

"I'm Barbara Mayfield," responded the stranger. "I just moved back here, but you might say I'm new too. I was living near Ft. Campbell, Kentucky, until my husband was killed in Iraq about a year ago."

"Oh my, I'm so sorry to hear that," said Lee Downs as he made note of her being single but trying not to appear overly anxious about wanting to get to know her better.

"I have not done much of anything here in Sassafras Springs. I need to get on with my life and get a job," began Barbara Mayfield. "I did join the church choir some weeks ago thanks to encouragement from Dollie Burgess. She had brought me some brownies to welcome me to the community and when she found I sang invited me to join the choir. I'll be meeting with them tonight. They have been very nice to me since I came back."

"Choir? You mean at the church on Nickerson Street?" replied Lee with surprise.

"Yes, that's the one."

"I was asked to be a part of that this morning and was leaning toward doing it. If you are in the choir I am sure it must be a good one. I'll definitely be there tonight," Lee said as he tried to flatter her as she made her way to the door.

He quickly grabbed a paper and pencil and looked up.

"Great, I'll see you there. What was your name?" he asked.

She didn't respond as she continued out the door.

"Lee was my name. And if I recall you are Barbara? Barbara? Is that right?"

She was gone. He hoped it was right and wrote it on the paper and placed it in his pocket. He also wrote "Nickerson Street Church choir practice Wednesday night" to make sure he didn't forget. He decided he was going to make a habit of being at the choir practice.

CHAPTER SIX

"This is Sherrie Bennett who does a wonderful job of playing the organ for church services," introduced Dollie Burgess. "She is so patient with us when we are rehearsing and have to go over the same section time and time again."

Sherrie stopped to look at the man Dollie was introducing and nodded with a friendly smile. "Sherrie, this is Lee Downs who is an intern this summer with Josh McDaniel at the newspaper."

Sherrie bowed again but was struggling to keep all of the music in her hands. Lee relieved her situation by taking the stack of slick covered music that had been under her arm. The slick covers made it almost uncontrollable. She laughed and said thank you as Dollie Burgess began introducing the next person in the room.

Lee Downs looked around to find Barbara but didn't see her. He took a seat in the bass section with a frown of disappointment.

"Don't tell me I came to work with this group for nothing," he thought.

"This is our director, Joan Stacy," continued Dollie Burgess with her introductions of everyone in the room.

"Joan is very talented. We are very lucky to have someone trained as well as she is in music."

"Joan, a pleasure to meet you," began Lee Downs smoothly to make a good impression. "Where did you study music?"

"I was a student at the Conservatory of Music in Pasadena, California, when a small girl and then attended the University of Missouri-Kansas City later," she responded.

"Indeed. Very nice. I look forward to your instruction and leadership."

Joan Stacy blushed and nodded as she went to the director's stand. She began unpacking her bag of music and started humming. Then she broke forth in "Ahhh-Eeee-Eyyyy-Ohhhh-Oooo" as the opening warm up drill. The choir responded and the rehearsal was underway. Lee Downs looked around and still did not see Barbara Mayfield.

"Do I have the right church?" he thought. He leaned over to Robert, one of the Stewart twins and asked, "Is this Nickerson Street Church?"

Robert laughed and verified it was Nickerson Street Church and the right location for the choir rehearsal. Lee was very disappointed. He had plans for the two of them. He wanted to begin by taking her out for a drink following the rehearsal. He was eager to see how good a singer she was as well.

Most of all, he was interested in hearing about her effort to get a job and what kind of experience she had. He was considering asking her to work for him on the newspaper staff if the newspapers sold as well as he thought they would.

"Barbara would be a great addition to the staff," he thought. "She seems more like a city girl than the others who I've met. I need a girl with new ideas and an appreciation of the ideas I have in mind for the local newspaper. She would agree that the little sleepy town of Sassafras Springs needs to be moved into the 21st century."

He looked around the room and reminded himself of the names he had been told by Dollie earlier. There was the deep voice of Steve Elsea. He had met Steve earlier in the day when Steve came by with an ad for the hardware store. He noticed the man's arm was bandaged and wondered what had happened.

There was Lincoln Madison who someone had said was a custodian at school. There was Margaret Cushing who he met the day Josh had the heart attack. Next to her sat Colleen Marx, Robert & Ralph Stewart, and several others. Finally there was Jessica Blandon who had hosted the birthday party and given him the front page news story. She waved at him when she came in and asked how the story turned out.

"Yes," laughed Steve Elsea. "I was working on repairing the broken window in the church sign and before I knew it the glass fell on my arm cutting it. I rushed to the hospital. Thankfully it wasn't a major cut. Just looked like it with blood spurting everywhere."

"Wow," remarked Lincoln Madison. "You are sure lucky. That could have been extremely serious."

Lee took his tablet out and jotted down some information. Looking the two men over he decided they would make an article for the newspaper. He could see the headline "Handyman Injured in Death Trap Church Building."

He scanned the building with his eyes for additional material to include in the article. He remembered the stairway and how it squeaked with every step he took coming to the choir loft. He continued to write on his tablet saying "risking the lives of the choir every rehearsal" and "the church unreasonably expects the members to sing and remain quiet about hidden dangers in the antiquated building."

"She stood right there and told me," said Colleen Marx. "She knew it was a lie. How could she tell me that?"

"Now, now," comforted Dollie Burgess. "Sometimes people don't always see things clearly. She probably was telling you the way she saw it. Try to see her side of it."

"Dollie," continued Colleen, "those people have intentions of hurting others with their big city attitudes."

"Hey, Maggie!" interrupted Dollie, "Jump in here anytime. Can you shine some light on this situation? You know the Harmons."

"What!" responded Margaret Cushing as she was deep in thought about the upcoming sale planned for her business the next day.

"The Harmons have upset Colleen the way they talk about the neighbors," explained Dollie Burgess. "Mrs. Harmon apparently said that her neighbor Andre Sanders should be deported before he starts his own lawn care business."

"What?" said Margaret Cushing amazed at what she had heard. "He already has one. Andre mows my yard and does a professional job. He charges the normal rate. What is wrong with him working for a living? The Harmons could learn a thing or two from the work ethics of Andre."

Lee smiled and went to writing another note. "These people are terrific! I can get a newspaper full of articles at every rehearsal. I'm glad I came to choir practice. Now let me see. 'Immigrants taking over job market in Sassafras Springs' and 'Class Struggle Developing in Neighborhood War.'"

Joan Stacy cleared her throat and looked at the group in order to get them quieted down. Then she started the warm up drill again. As the group started a sound was heard below them.

A slow step by step squeak could be heard as someone made their way up the stairs to where the group was seated in the choir loft. Lee twisted to see who it was. He was not disappointed. It was Barbara. She was late, but she was there.

The rehearsal went very well and he admitted to himself that the choir was good at singing and perfecting everything that Joan selected. The group prepared two numbers for the following Sunday morning church service. It then occurred to Lee that he would need to attend church services if he was going to be in the choir.

"Well, if Barbara is there," he thought, "I won't mind attending church every Sunday."

At the end of the rehearsal while he was being measured for a choir robe by Dollie Burgess, Barbara Mayfield made her way to Lee's side and said, "Did you enjoy the rehearsal? The choir is pretty good for a small town choir."

"Yes they are good and yes I did enjoy it," he replied, "but I would not have enjoyed it as much without you being here."

"You think?" said Barbara as she blushed and laughed at his attempt to flatter her. Dollie paused from inserting pins in the hem of the choir robe and looked at the two. She smiled and chuckled to herself.

"Love is in the air," she thought. "How sweet...."

Lee ducked his head slightly, took a deep breath and then asked Barbara to join him for a drink at the Crème Maid around the corner. She accepted and the two left talking and smiling as they were on their way chatting and getting to know each other.

CHAPTER SEVEN

"Hi, Ike," began Rev. Temple as he entered Porter's Place. "I was passing by and saw your special sign in the window. Do you mean you are having dried apple pies today? That's my favorite."

"You bet we do," answered Ike. "We got a gift of six gallon dried apples from Ollie Ditty yesterday. She apparently had a bumper crop of apples and has done everything she can with them. She thought we might like her recipe for fried dried apple pies and gave us some dried apples to practice making the pies."

The smell of apples and nutmeg filled the restaurant and it wasn't long before the entire restaurant was filled with people not able to resist the smell enticing them to come in the restaurant for a taste. The place was packed with people eating and enjoying their early morning pie and coffee when Lee stopped by with a load of newspapers.

"Get your morning paper to enjoy with that delicious smelling pie. Wow! What is that?" asked Lee Down.

"Fried dried apple pies," replied Rev. Temple waving

and motioning for Lee to join him. "Believe me they are delicious."

"No time today. I'm eager to get the newspapers on the street and planning to go by and see Mr. McDaniel this morning too," replied Lee Downs.

"I see you got the newspaper done," said Rev. Temple as he motioned with a dollar bill to come over and he would buy one. On the way to Rev. Temple's table, Lee sold six others.

The crowd was soon buzzing about the front page articles. As Lee made his way back across the room another six newspapers were sold. Obviously his headlines were getting a response and others were anxious to get the whole story.

"Who would have believed that sweet woman was an arsonist?" said one reader.

"Who? Where did you see that?" asked another.

"Jessica Blandon did what?" said another stunned reader.

"I don't believe any of this," stated one individual. "Wow, there are pictures to prove it. Look at that fire!!!"

"Just the other day she and I were talking about her daughter's birthday party. Who would have believed she would go off and do something like this?" added another.

"What kind of animal is that and why hasn't someone killed it?" cried one lady.

"Wait just a minute. Did you read the whole article?" said Rev. Temple. "Lee?"

Lee was out the door. His job was done. The newspapers were selling like hotcakes and the money was rolling in. He could report to Josh McDaniel that things were going quite well at the newspaper.

The crowd was talking louder when Margaret Cushing entered. She edged her way to Rev. Temple's table and sat down as she looked around at the packed café. Everyone was intently reading their newspaper. She greeted Rev. Temple and not getting a response she tapped him on the head.

"Ah-hum," she began. "Jack--Jack? Jack?"

"Oh, Margaret…," said Rev. Temple when he finally realized she was talking to him. "I'm sorry. I was reading this morning's rather remarkable newspaper."

"So, Lee Downs managed to get it out on time. Well, maybe I was wrong about him," she replied.

"Not necessarily," replied Rev. Temple. "I'm not sure what to think at this point."

"What do you mean? What's wrong?"

Rev. Temple handed her the newspaper and a few seconds later her mouth dropped open and she was staring in disbelief at Rev. Temple.

"Did you read this?" Margaret Cushing asked.

"Yes," replied Rev. Temple.

"Jessica Blandon is an arsonist? I don't believe it. What did she do?" Margaret Cushing asked.

"Read the entire article. It is continued on page 11 hidden below the cartoons---where no one will see it," responded Rev. Temple.

"But----?" said a near speechless Margaret Cushing.

"Yes, you would think Jessica was a totally wild woman," interrupted Ike Winston as he stopped to refill their coffee cups. "Running around setting fire to buildings, humiliating her daughter, and endangering the lives of the entire neighborhood until you get to the last paragraph when you find she was simply lighting the candles on her daughter's birthday cake. What was that new guy thinking when he wrote this article?"

"Selling newspapers I would guess and they are selling fast," said Rev. Temple.

The whole restaurant was in an uproar with the vocally

aroused and angry citizens about this "dangerous woman." The readers grumbled louder and louder. They began expressing hopes that this evil woman had been arrested. The crowd got even louder when Officer Hays came in for his break for coffee and a donut.

"Officer Hays, good! We want to know what you are going to do about this wild arsonist on the loose in Sassafras Springs?" asked one reader of the newspaper.

"I'm sorry. I'm not familiar with that situation. What are you talking about?" replied the Officer who was immediately handed a newspaper to read.

"You know!" said another reader standing and pounding the top of a table demanding that justice be done. "This Jessica Blandon is running around town setting fire to people's homes! I heard she was going to be prosecuted for that fire over in Shanghai."

"Did you read the entire story? There is more to it on page 11 and you need to read it before you start making accusations or start getting a rope to hang this poor woman," said Rev. Temple. "Think people! Read the entire story."

The sound of newspaper pages being turned could be heard as some sought to know more. Then one by one groans of displeasure could be heard as individually the readers reached the end of the article on page 11.

"Well, isn't that a disappointment," said one reader. "I was looking forward to a trial and being able to gossip about someone in town doing something awful."

"Yeah, what a disappointment," groaned another.

"Well, I tell you she was up for arson in Shanghia before the tornado hit that town. That is why she moved here. She wanted to get away from the cops. They were about to crack the case wide open and arrest her."

"Where in the world did you come up with that information?" asked Rev. Temple.

"He made it up," spouted off Margaret Cushing. "That man constantly stirs up gossip in this community. You are a bad man. How could you say things about that sweet Jessica? You probably don't even know her."

With the conversation getting louder Margaret Cushing and Rev. Temple decided to leave. The atmosphere was getting pretty unpleasant. Talk was getting ugly.

Once outside the café, Margaret excused herself saying she was going to visit Jessica Blandon to give her some support in case some of the people in town really believed the idea that she was an arsonist. Rev. Temple patted her on the back and agreed that was a good idea. He decided he would track down Lee Downs and find out what the intentions were with the article. Pulling out from his parking place Rev. Temple remembered that Lee had mentioned he was going to visit Josh McDaniel. He turned his car in the direction of the hospital.

CHAPTER EIGHT

"Would the council meeting come to order?" requested Mayor Rick Wallingford as he sounded his gavel and called the city council to take their seats at the conference table. "There is a lot of business to handle tonight and I'm eager to get things started."

Hearing the sound of the gavel Lee Downs ran from the parking lot to get a seat and was delighted to find one on the front row. He set his tape recorder on the chair next to him and turned it on. Next he prepared his camera and arranged it on the chair so he could quickly pick it up if he needed to take a picture. Finally he took a tablet of paper and began writing.

The community building conference room had four rows of seats with six in each row. There was a speaker's stand in the center of the two 8 foot folding tables set across the front of the room. Sitting at the tables were the six board members and the mayor along with the city clerk who was taking notes. Normally the audience would consist of four to six people. There would be the city manager, city police chief along with Johnny Burkhart who was in charge of the Civil Defense in town. Occasionally, the district fire chief would be present as the council was working on a grant to obtain a new fire station. Tonight, much to the surprise of Lee, the place was packed with some 20 additional people.

His mind raced working to think of something that would be headline news from this meeting. "What can I do to stir things up and get a story?" he thought.

As was the tradition the minutes and treasurer's reports were presented and approved by the council. Old business was discussed which included talk about overgrown yards not being mowed resulting in snakes and other smaller animals nesting in the tall grass. Reports were presented by the city police chief concerning the attempt to get broken down cars and parts removed from residential properties.

Other discussion dealt with the water system and the need to replace plastic pipes with new improved pipes. A debate on purchasing a new water pump for the city was once again brought to the table and tabled for lack of money and failure to get more than one bid for replacing the pump.

New business included the Fair Board's request for an easement to sell beer in a beer garden at the fair to be setup and maintained by the fair board as a fundraiser. Every year the effort was stopped by the minister's alliance but this year the fair board had new support for the beer garden from the mayor. He had attended the St. Cloud Fair and saw firsthand the advantages of controlling the beer drinking in a closed area.

The discussion once again was heated concerning the beer as citizen after citizen approached the microphone to voice their opinion. Later questions were encouraged from the audience as the council made every effort to hear from all of those present. Everyone was surprised when the new reporter for the newspaper stood and went to the microphone to ask a question.

"Mr. Mayor," he began. "I see you are favoring the beer request by the Fair Board this year. Is that correct, Sir?"

The mayor appeared confident in his response. He once again voiced his views. He responded that he had not changed his position. At a request by the reporter, the mayor quickly summarized his position one last time.

"Yes, I plan to vote in support of the beer garden," the mayor replied.

"Then tell us, sir. Did you or did you not enter a rehab hospital ten years ago while living in another community?" forcefully asked Lee.

The mayor's mouth dropped open just as Lee quickly took his camera and shot a picture of the mayor's appearance.

"Of course not," the mayor responded. "I have never had a drop of liquor in my life."

"Is that true? Or are you determined to cover up your past of heavy drinking and abuse of your family while drunk?" Lee persisted.

"What are you talking about? I have never had a drop of liquor in my life. This is out of order. Are there any more questions from the floor?" said the mayor as he attempted to get Lee away from the microphone.

"Wait Mr. Mayor, I am not finished with my question. Is it true that the local brewery offered you money last weekend if you would support approval of this easement for the Fair Board? Is it true that you accepted a bribe?"

The crowd gasped. Several began mumbling and voicing a desire to hear an answer from the mayor. Several began raising hands to get the opportunity to ask questions. The mayor laughed and said, "Man, I don't know who your sources are but you need new ones."

Lee snapped another picture of the mayor as he was laughing and trying to pass over the questions. The mayor attempted to get the discussion back on the matter of the beer garden by announcing the date for the fair and how important it was to make a decision at the meeting. The minister's alliance members were adamant about the need to postpone the vote until all the issues were dealt with. The Sassafras Springs Fair Board was just as demanding that a vote be taken as they needed to make arrangements for the garden construction and beer deliveries. Waiting another month for the next board meeting would cause them to not have enough time to be able to be ready for the summer fair.

"Mr. Mayor, we have to have a vote tonight," demanded the Fair Board president.

"Mayor Wallingford, we demand you not vote tonight or you'll find the minister's calling for your resignation in their church services Sunday."

The mayor looked at the frowning faces of the crowd. He could hear them growling and whispering to each other with all sorts of accusations. He finally looked at his fellow councilmen and asked, "Is there a motion to adjourn before this dissolves into a physical fight?"

Councilman Reynolds raised his hand and said, "Aye, adjournment please."

Mayor Wallingford then quickly said, "There is a motion to adjourn. All in favor say 'aye.'"

Councilmen unanimously said, "Aye!" as the audience booed.

The meeting adjourned as several members circled around Lee and praised him for his bravery in confronting the mayor with the accusations.

"We need to know these things. We count on the press to inform us of the truth about these politicians who try to steal our money and spend it on themselves."

"Yeah," added another individual. "It is all a plot by the liquor industry to persuade our kids to drink. They got to the mayor and we needed to know that before he allowed this issue to be approved. We must keep our kids from public drinking and a beer garden will send the wrong message."

"Wait," broke in a Fair Board member. "This issue is not dead. We will get it passed this year because the mayor saw what we saw a long time ago. If drinking is going to go on at the Friday night dance it ought to be contained in an area where the police are located to keep a stabbing from taking place like it did last year."

"Hey, then don't have liquor. That is how you keep from having stabbings or fights."

"Lee," began Rev. Temple, "what do you have in mind with this information you dumped on the city tonight? Do you have any evidence that this is true? I have known the mayor rather well since I arrived here and I can't imagine him attacking his wife or children like you said. I have never seen him drink. I tend to believe that he is telling the truth when he says he has never drank."

"Did he go to college," asked Lee.

"He has a master's degree from the University of Western Military," replied Jack.

"Well, there you are," laughed Lee. "If he went to UWM he undoubtedly drank. How could you be a part of that party school without drinking every weekend? You bet he drank and from there went on to abuse his family."

"Lee?" continued Jack. "Do you have any evidence of this? I want the truth? You are destroying a man's political career. Be careful what you are doing if this is not true. Lee? Come back. I want to know. I have to know."

Lee quickly packed his things and disappeared out the side entrance. He had pictures and his story for the front page of the next day's newspaper. This would sell more newspapers than the previous issue. He could hardly contain his joy as he started his car and pulled away from the parking lot.

He drove to the newspaper office and then decided he should go to a motel in a neighboring city to set up the information with his laptop. "Avoiding crowds at the moment might be a good idea," he thought.

Remembering that Sherry had resigned over concern about the articles he was including in the newspaper and how he left facts out and sensationalized simple stories, he began thinking about how he would find a replacement for her.

"Wonder if that new girl, Barbara, would take a job typing for the newspaper? That would be nice to have her at the office all day."

Meanwhile, Rev. Temple was cornered by the other ministers of the community who all agreed that they should unite in calling for the mayor's resignation. Rev. Temple asked them to consider the evidence presented by Lee Downs. Rev. Temple pointed out that Lee had only made statements and had no proof. There was no evidence for what he blatantly added to the discussion.

"Lee is new in town and could not possibly have learned this information in such a short time," added Rev. Temple as he begged them to hold off calling for a petition drive until the facts were known.

Despite his pleas the Minister's Alliance voted to call for their congregations to sign petitions the following Sunday.

CHAPTER NINE

"Good evening everyone," said Lee as he entered the loft for choir practice. The group looked at him and nodded and then looked away. They instead looked at each other, frowned, and mumbled words under their breath. The group continued to be totally silent except for Joan who occasionally gave direction to the organist of what songs would be used during the rehearsal. Simple glances at each other by the choir members echoed silently the messages on each of their minds and as much as they wanted to say something they knew they didn't dare start.

Finally, Dollie Burgess went over to Lee and said, "Mr. Downs, you are new here and it might do you well to understand that we care about our neighbors and friends. You attacked unfairly one of our very own choir members. Jessica is not here tonight because of how you embarrassed her in the newspaper."

"Why, I don't understand," he firmly said. "The stories were all true. I grant the headlines did get your attention but everything I wrote was true. It is my job to sell newspapers. It is a business and sometimes you need to write things in a way to grab people---to get them to stop their rushing around thru a day and to take a look at the news in their community."

"I'm sure there is a way to do that without destroying a person," responded Dollie Burgess. "but you have hurt Jessica deeply."

"Surely you are exaggerating," replied Lee Downs. "I told the truth in the article and gave her lots of publicity on the party she had. They ought to thank me for writing the article about their get together."

A loud grown could be heard as the entire group rolled their eyes and changed positions to look away from the man.

Dollie Burgess shrugged her shoulders and went back to her place. She only knew that her friend Jessica Blandon had been hurt deeply and it would take some time for Jessica to recover from the mean spirited phone calls and the people driving by her house yelling horrible things. This simple news article Lee had printed had turned Jessica's life upside down.

"Barbara, over here," hollered Lee Downs as Barbara Mayfield entered the loft. "I want to talk to you before the rehearsal begins."

Barbara Mayfield quickly hurried to his side with a smile on her face and greeted him. He was pleased to see a friendly face after being so coldly received by the others.

"Did you see the newspaper today?" he asked.

She nodded negatively and moved over to the soprano section as Joan Stacy was behind the roster taking deep breaths signaling they were about to start. The choir was quickly harmonizing various syllables as the vocal exercises began.

Lee waved his hand to get the attention of Barbara and then motioned he wanted to take her to the Crème Maid again for a drink. She smiled and sent an agreeable look back with a wink. Lee's heart was pounding as he stared at the beautiful woman he was beginning to get to know. He would ask her to work as his typist tonight.

"It would be very nice to have her around the office," he thought. "I hope she accepts."

"Alice," began Rev. Leonard Hollywood of the Back Street Gospel Church of Fire as they unloaded a table and chairs at the SuperMart Shopping Center, "Did you bring the signs?"

"Yes, Rev. Lenny," she replied as she handed a huge box to him.

"What's this?" asked Rev. Hollywood.

"The petitions you ordered. We can circulate around the downtown and probably come up with a hundred or more signers on the petition before noon."

"Good work," cheered Rev. Hollywood. "We need more enthusiastic workers like you if we are going to replace that good for nothing mayor."

The minister, Rev. Leonard Hollywood, was one of those televangelist types who dressed with a rose in his lapel and smelled of cologne. You could smell him coming a block away. He was good looking with a strut in his walk that immediately notified you that this man thought he was God sent to lead the lost to salvation.

His wife, Maria Rose, was covered with makeup and always fluttering her eyes with the extra large fake eyelashes. Even though she was from south St. Louis she spoke with a Georgia drawl that was about as fake as her eyelashes. When she walked she had a twist in her hips that attracted every man she passed. These two "holy people" strongly believed it was their mission to bring the mayor to his knees in confession for the evil deeds he was reported to have done.

"Mabel," yelled Alice across the parking lot. "Wait up! I have something to show you."

Alice was one of Rev. Hollywood's finest supporters and workers. She was always out to knock down the proud and pull the rug out from under the leaders. She knew anyone in power needed to be replaced. Didn't matter the party, the political connections or whether they were right or wrong. It was her job, she thought, to make sure everyone was showing respect for Rev. and Mrs. Hollywood and following their leadership. Rev. Hollywood had preached about the need to replace the mayor and she was going to make sure that happened.

"Alice," responded Mabel when she reached Alice's side. "What's going on here?"

"The mayor---you know he is a drug dealer and rumor has it killed some man before he moved her....something about union business," began Alice.

"The mayor," said Mabel in astonishment. "But---? That can't be. I play cards with his wife and she is a wonderful person. Where did you get this information?"

"At the city council meeting last Monday night," reported Alice. "He denied ever having anything to do with drugs. Denied anything to do with missing money. Denied knowing some convict from Mississippi."

"Convict from Mississippi? Where does he come into this?"

Alice was making up most of the story as she continued but she was determined to get Mabel to carry one of their signs around the parking lot. Mabel on the other hand wanted to know the truth but found the entire situation beyond her comprehension. She finally decided to disappear into the store to shop with hopes that Alice would be gone when she returned.

"Sally," said Alice as she spotted another friend. "Giving

away kittens again? You know you need to get your cats fixed. Seems like you are down here all the time giving away kittens."

"Hi, Alice," replied Sally from the back of her truck holding a couple of the cutest gray and white kittens. You could hear their little mews as Sally rubbed their heads. "These aren't my kittens. They were left on my doorstep and well, I couldn't take them. I decided to bring them down to give away. Always some children here who need a cat or two to liven up their lives."

"Sure thing, but none for me today!" said Alice.

"So what cause are you out to solve or conquer today," asked Sally knowing that Alice was always out for blood or to bring someone to justice. Alice's reputation had become well known as one who you don't want to make mad. Her long line of successes and victories on overthrowing people of power had been proven long ago.

Alice was six feet tall and her arms revealed muscles made from chopping wood for her wood stove. She believed the world was destroying itself with fossil fuels and was determined to use only wood. The fact that the wood emitted gases had seemingly failed to register with her. She made a huge garden insisting that people needed to go back to natural foods that don't have those bug sprays on them. She cut the grass in her yard with a non-electric push type mower. There was no air conditioning in her house. She insisted that the windows be open for fresh air. Her cabinets were filled with three months of groceries insisting that the country would be in civil war soon.

By 11 a.m. Alice had managed to get a dozen people to carry signs and another half dozen with clipboards asking people to sign petitions. Rev. Hollywood and his wife had left saying they would work the other side of town not mentioning that both of them had appointments at the Glamour-Spa for a haircut and manicure.

About noon, two other ministers arrived and set up camp to seek others to sign petitions as the effort continued to grow. The momentum by 1 p.m. had produced 300 signatures on the petitions. Most of the signatures were by people out of town who were not registered voters for the city, but the workers were very proud and decided to continue working throughout the afternoon until they had doubled the number.

Around 2:30, Lee Downs stopped by and took pictures of the demonstrators with their signs and petitions. He was eager to get another newspaper on the streets showing the effect of his questions at the council meeting. He did a quick count of the names on the petitions and expressed that the group should turn them into the City Clerk before 5 p.m. that day so he could print that a recall had been made on the mayor.

"Good morning, Rev. Temple. I'm glad to see you," began the mayor. "I hear you are the only preacher in town that didn't call for my resignation Sunday. You would think the ministers of Sassafras Springs would want to check the facts and know the truth before jumping on the band wagon to have me ousted. I appreciate that you believed in me enough to want some facts."

"That's what I came for," began Rev. Temple. "Tell me the facts, Rick."

"I don't know what to tell you except I never drink, never abused my family and am a peace loving man. I certainly didn't take a bribe from the brewery. I only supported the beer garden because I wanted to insure that the drinking was in a controlled area and there wouldn't be any fighting like last year. It seemed simple enough when I explained my position."

"Yes," began Rev. Temple. "It was very well explained and although I disagree with your view I certainly do understand and appreciate your desire to see order and safety for the fair."

The mayor turned away from the door and walked to the couch in his living room. Rev. Temple followed and quickly took a seat near the center of the room. He opened the notebook and pulled out a pen and was preparing to write. He looked straight at the mayor and tried to look deep inside of him.

The mayor appeared nervous, but in control. He started to sit on the couch but chose to take one of the chairs by the fireplace. The chair had a big angel winged back. The upholstery was white with dark blue stripes. It matched another one on the other side of the room. The two chairs flanked the fireplace. Above the fireplace was a picture of the mayor and his wife. At the side of the room was a table in front of the windows that displayed a bouquet of flowers. Rev. Temple could smell the fresh flowers from where he sat. Against the wall on both sides of the fireplace were bookshelves loaded with books and photographs of the family.

The place felt warm and safe. Rev. Temple looked at the mayor and then smiled at him to give him encouragement. Despite the friendly surroundings there was a moment of uncomfortable silence.

"Let's face facts, mayor. If we are going to find a solution for this situation we need God on our side so let's pray," suggested Rev. Temple.

"Please do Rev. Temple," responded the mayor as he bowed his head.

"Precious Father, please open our eyes that we may understand what the purpose of this situation is. Father, guide the mayor as he makes decisions and help us to work to bring the truth out on this issue. Lead us to the answers we need and strengthen the mayor and his family as they endure these attacks. We pray these things in the name of Jesus Christ, our Savior, amen."

The two men sat quietly while Rev. Temple made some notes in his notebook. The sound of the wind outside could be heard. The limb of a shrub was striking the window and making a scratching sound. In a short time they could hear rain hitting the window.

"The weatherman hit it right today," remarked Rev. Temple to open conversation.

"I thought it wouldn't rain today because they said it would," laughed the mayor. "Seems like if they say it will it doesn't and if they say it won't it does."

Rev. Temple nodded and laughed. Again he smiled at the mayor and began writing.

"Jack, what have you got in mind?" asked the mayor as he could see there was a bit of a twinkle in Rev. Temple's eyes. "I know that look. Much like when you were planning on getting me to judge the pie eating contest at the church bazaar. Do you have a plan?"

"You know me pretty well," began Rev. Temple, "just as I know you and I know you are an honest man. When you say you don't drink or abuse your family I believe you. I have confidence in what you are saying so let's get to work on finding something we can do to get this situation cleared up."

The mayor looked Rev. Temple over with an appreciative look. He considered the young bachelor preacher a friend though they were in different social circles. Rick Wallingford wrinkled his brow with curiosity as he examined the possibilities of what ideas Rev. Temple might have to solve the problem. The mayor had already considered a number of ideas but had decided all of them would only make things worse. He shrugged his shoulders and sighed. It was hopeless from his standpoint trying to combat the accusations and rumors flying over the community.

"Jack, I don't think there is anything," said the mayor weakly. "I have given 10 years to this community in public service. I have volunteered for numerous projects. I have donated regularly to the various charities. I attend and support the church, yet one rumor destroyed me."

"Maybe not," hinted Rev. Temple.

Rev. Temple fumbled thru the pages of his notepad and settled onto one particular page. He took his pen and began writing again. Mayor Wallingford quietly watched as Rev. Temple left his chair and walked to the wall of honors the mayor had received. Jack began reading the words on the diplomas and awards displayed.

There on the wall was a plaque honoring Mayor Wallingford for his service on a city council in another community. Rev. Temple copied the dates and other information from the plaque and then looked at the next. This plaque honored Mr. Wallingford for a number of years of service and for retirement from the company. Next was a plaque the mayor had received from the unions for his assistance in helping the working men and women get higher salaries and health benefits.

"You are obviously dedicated to helping others. One glance over the wall of honors and you look like a pretty nice man determined to make sure your fellow men and women are treated right and fairly."

"Well, that reporter was here and he didn't seem

impressed. He was actually irritated with the plaques," said the mayor.

"What do you mean?" asked Rev. Temple with a surprised look on his face. "Why was he looking at them? Was there one that he particularly looked at?"

"Why, yes I believe there was?" replied the mayor. "Let me think. I believe it was the one from the unions. He even made a groaning sound which almost sounded like he was angry. Yes, he was obviously annoyed that I had that. I can't imagine why. At the time everyone was supportive and happy for me--well, except for Jackson Coleman."

"Jackson Coleman?"

"Yes, Jackson Coleman," the mayor continued. "He and I were officers with the labor union back then. He was treasurer and I had to report that he was pocketing money from the dues turned in by the members. It caused quite a scandal. Jackson insisted I had set him up and I was never sure what the situation was. He could have been set up but the fact was that he had deposits in the bank of the amounts that were missing from the treasury."

"Jackson Coleman?" continued Jack in his investigation. "Do you know where he is now?"

"I assume he is in jail," replied the mayor. "He was arrested and the evidence was pretty strong. I did have questions about the matter because he didn't seem like the type to steal. He even introduced me to Mollie, my wife, at a dinner at his house. I have something in my office files. Follow me and we'll look for the folder. "

The mayor led Rev. Temple to the west side of the house and entered a room surrounded with books and a large desk in the center. There was a computer, telephone, shelves and filing cabinets. Inside the cabinets were duplicate records for reference at home when the mayor was not at the city hall. Another stack of files was on the side of his desk that he had brought home from the city hall that morning when it became apparent he could not work at the office.

"And what type of person do you think would steal?" asked Rev. Temple.

"Good point," mumbled the mayor as he began shuffling thru a drawer. "Guess you can never tell who will be a thief or embezzler."

The mayor shut the first drawer and began pulling drawer after drawer in his office going thru files and pulling out folders.

"Here it is!" declared the mayor.

"What do you have there?" responded Rev. Temple.

"This is my file on the entire investigation. I did my own investigation at the time and there were a lot of things that did not add up."

"Like what?"

"Well, there was another name that kept popping up who was someone working for the company. Certainly wasn't a member of the union. I can't remember the name. It should be here."

The mayor continued to sort thru the file when Rev. Temple spotted an obituary. It was for Leonard Downright. He pulled it out of the side of the file and began reading.

"Leonard Downright, 44, of south of this community died yesterday when he fell from scaffolding at the construction site for the American Labor Unions new headquarters on Judson Street. Downright leaves his wife, Millie (Coleman) Downright of the home; one son, Leonard Downright, Jr. and wife of Arnold; and his parents, Mr. & Mrs. Winston Downright of Sassafras Springs, Missouri."

"Did you see this, mayor? Do you know these people?" asked Rev. Temple.

"Downright? Hummmm. Yes, that was the one I was

trying to think of. He was apparently involved in a financial investment plan with Jackson. They said it was going to produce 8 percent interest and the money placed in Jackson's account was invested with that financial plan," explained the mayor.

"So, did you find that to be true or what was the story," Rev. Temple questioned.

"Downwright died too soon for us to pursue his connection. The Sheriff's Department dropped him as a suspect and they were sure they had the right man with Coleman. As I said, there was a lot of concrete evidence to support the idea that Coleman had stolen the money."

"Do you suppose this Downwright is related to Jackson Coleman as the paper lists his wife's maiden name as Coleman?" asked Rev. Temple.

"What do you mean?"

"I'm just trying to get all the facts," continued Rev. Temple. "Did Lee Downs ask you any other questions?"

"Not anything other than the regular questions you would expect him to ask," responded Mayor Wallingford. "Wait a minute. I do remember wondering in my mind about why he was asking so many questions about the union. Also I wondered where he had gotten his information as it seemed like he knew more than would be public knowledge."

"Well, that could explain a lot of things," replied Rev. Temple. "Any ideas of why he would know more than the general public?"

"Of course not," paused Mayor Wallingford. "Here is a thought. We all called Leonard Downwright by the name of Lee. He didn't like Leonard as a name. Do you suppose this Lee is the son of Leonard Downwright who died at the construction site?"

"No, the reporter's last name is Downs-----that is

remarkably close to the same name though. There might be more here than meets the eye. Might be worth checking."

There was a pause in the conversation as they both took a moment to examine other information and clippings in the file.

"Another question I have is about whether Downwright died of natural causes or was he killed?" asked Rev. Temple as he was beginning to become intensely interested in what they were finding.

"I don't have a clue," sighed the mayor. "This has brought a lot of bad memories back as it was very ugly and extremely difficult for me to work with the prosecution against Coleman. I really liked him. I still am not sure he stole the money or was stealing it. He insisted he didn't know how the money got in his account. When we showed him the statement he said it was the first he knew of the deposits. I wanted to believe him."

"Yes, there are a lot of strange things here," agreed Rev. Temple. "I'm going to get Officer Hays to help. I know he feels like I do---that you are innocent---and maybe this political hatchet job can be stopped. Lee Downs appears to be determined to sell newspapers at all costs to the people around him. He doesn't seem to care whether he prints the truth or not. It won't hurt to examine him too."

"Thanks Jack," said the mayor as he patted Rev. Temple on the back. "I appreciate your help though I suspect there isn't much we can do about the rumors flying over the town. I might as well resign and move on with my life."

"Not yet, mayor," requested Rev. Temple. "Let me do some checking first. I think there is a lot more to this story than we know."

The two men walked back into the living room. As Rev. Temple was gathering his notebook and taking one more glance at the plaques he stopped and starred at the portrait of the mayor and his wife.

"She was a beautiful bride in that picture," remarked Rev. Temple.

"Yes she was," smiled the mayor. "I think she has gotten more beautiful every year. We met in Arnold, Missouri, shortly after this whole mess developed with the union dues and instantly we fell in love. We were married a week later and moved to O'Fallon."

"That is where you served on the city council before moving here. Is that right?" asked Rev. Temple.

"Yes it is," replied the mayor. "I believe you would make a good detective. Nothing gets by you."

CHAPTER TEN

"Hi, Jack," started Josh McDaniel. "Did you come to take me home?"

"Home?" exclaimed Rev. Temple. "Did the doctors say you could go home already? That's great news Josh!"

"No," sighed Josh McDaniel. "Just wishful thinking on my part I'm afraid. They are checking me out for possible surgery. They said there is considerable blockage that needs to be taken care of before I return home."

Josh McDaniel adjusted the IV tube in his wrist and shifted his body to the other side to get a better view of Rev. Temple.

"That sounds serious," said Rev. Temple as he debated about telling Josh McDaniel what had happened at his newspaper. "So, you need to remain stress free?"

"Frankly, I need some excitement," laughed Josh McDaniel. "I'm going nuts in here I'm so bored. Say, how is my intern doing with the newspaper? He hasn't called or come by. I guess he has his hands full running everything. I did get a 'get-well' card from the staff."

Rev. Temple looked Josh McDaniel squarely in the face and decided he had to inform Josh what was happening with the newspaper. Rev. Temple mulled over how to explain it to Josh and then remembered there were copies of the newspapers in the car.

"Josh, I'll be right back. I have copies of the newspapers in the car and you can judge for yourself how he is doing."

"That sounds like he must be doing a great job. You think the town wants me to retire and turn the newspaper over to Lee? It probably looks better than it ever has and is more interesting. They said at the university he was a dynamic and outstanding journalism student."

"Don't be silly. You are totally wrong. Everyone is eagerly awaiting your return to work. They all care about you so get well quick. We are hoping you are back at your job as soon as possible. We miss you. Now be patient and I'll be right back and you can judge for yourself."

Rev. Temple disappeared and headed for the car. On the way out the front door of the hospital he met Dollie Burgess coming with a bouquet of some of her gladiolas directly from her garden. They were beautiful and smelled with a strong fragrance.

"Those are beautiful," remarked Rev. Temple. "Josh is sure to appreciate those. Aha! And I see a Tupperware container of probably some delicious treats of yours."

She nodded. Dollie was an excellent cook and her baked goods were a specialty for any occasion. She opened the container and offered a brownie to Rev. Temple. He quickly took one and started eating. He then thanked her and expressed how good it was and how much it reminded him of his grandmother's brownies.

When Dollie asked where he was going in such a hurry he grimaced and explained that he was on his way to the car to get copies of the newspapers for Josh. Dollie immediately shook her head and commented that she thought it was a bad idea to let Josh see them. The two discussed it for a few minutes and finally they both agreed the town couldn't handle much more of Lee Downs as editor. He had half the people fighting with each other already.

Dollie Burgess continued down the hospital hallway to Josh's room while Rev. Temple went to the car. By the time he got back Josh McDaniel appeared to have fallen asleep from the medication and Dollie Burgess had taken up residence in the big comfortable chair the hospital had provided for her the first night Josh was there.

"Sh-h-h-h," she motioned with her finger across her lips to insure Rev. Temple remained quiet. "He's asleep. I suggest we wait a little bit to show him the newspapers."

"You're right as always," Rev. Temple replied, "but we have to do something. You know we do. Lee Downs is tearing up the town."

For a few seconds Dollie Burgess and Rev. Temple were silent just looking at each other. Finally each one of them took a newspaper and began to reread the articles. They shook their heads and started mumbling about the trouble the articles had caused. They began to whisper angrily about what Lee had done to Jessica Blandon and to the mayor. Back and forth they expressed their deep concern and intense desire to bring a stop to the madness.

"Dollie, let's face it. The newspaper is the watch dog of society, but this watch dog in Sassafras Springs is foaming at the mouth. Under Lee's leadership the watch dog is mad!"

A groan could be heard from the bed. They both looked with panic thinking Josh might be having a heart attack, but were relieved when they saw one eye was open and he was staring at the newspaper in Jack's hand.

"MAYOR DENYS HE IS ALCOHOLIC? Where did that story come from? I've known the mayor for a long time and I know he doesn't drink. What is that about? And oh my gosh.....CITYWIDE PETITION DRIVE TO REMOVE

MAYOR? Ok, you two. Tell me what is happening. This can't be good."

The two gave him the newspapers and let him read thru the articles before answering any questions. Josh set up straighter as he made his way thru the newspapers. He was in shock as he saw all the work he had done to help bring the town together suddenly disappearing thanks to these issues of his newspaper.

"Just how much damage has he done to the mayor?" began Josh. "It can't be good. How is Mayor Wallingford holding up?"

"I just came from there and he seems to be dealing with it in the only way he knows how," reported Rev. Temple. "He was going to resign but I begged him to hold off on that for a bit. We have started gathering information to see if there is a reason that Lee Downs would attack the mayor. So far it seems just like an attempt to sell newspapers and that's it----at the cost of innocent people I might add."

Josh shook his head back and forth. He was mortified that his newspaper had these articles in them.

"Do you know anything about Leonard Downwright who was killed at the construction site that the mayor was working on before he came here?" questioned Rev. Temple. "When Lee Downs was at the mayor's he seemed interested in the union plaques and according to the mayor made some groans and came across like he was angry."

"That is disturbing," replied Josh as he considered the situation. "I can't say I remember that case. Was that here?"

"No, it was in Arnold, Missouri."

"Hummm," paused Josh. "I grew up in Arnold, but of course a kid doesn't pay much attention to those kinds of things."

"We also found that Jackson Coleman was arrested and

imprisoned for embezzlement of funds from the labor union treasury," continued Rev. Temple. "He was a brother-in-law of Leonard's and that both were possibly involved in the scandal. When Downwright was killed he was dropped from the investigation. The mayor was president of the labor union at the time and was originally accused. It was only for a short time as the information gathered by the police all pointed toward Coleman."

"Well, the plot thickens doesn't it?" responded Josh. "Do you have proof of this? We must have proof before sharing this with the public. Make sure you have the facts. Do you think this hatchet job by Lee has something to do with this man's death?"

"Not yet but a surprising twist occurred. Lee apparently doesn't know that Barbara Mayfield is the daughter of the mayor. He hired her as the typist replacing Sherry Martin so we have an inside way to find what stories are coming next in the newspaper."

"Sherry? What happened to Sherry?" asked Josh.

"She quit after the first issue. She said she didn't believe you would ever print stories like those about the arson and rioting children. She was horrified at the ridiculous way Lee manipulated the information to make sensational headlines."

"Rioting children? Did you say arson?" he exclaimed. "Whatever are you talking about? I can't imagine either in this town. What was set fire?"

"Here," Rev. Temple handed him the first newspaper to see the headlines. "Jessica Blandon was having a birthday party for her daughter and that was the party you were headed for when you had the heart attack."

"Oh yes, I remember now. I suddenly had those streaking pains going up my arms----," he said grimacing at the memories. "Let's not talk about those."

The room was quiet as Josh read thru the article. His eyes got big as he turned to page eleven where he found the story changed. He grunted and then tensed.

"Jessica lit the candles on top of the birthday cake? That was her horrible arsonist act?" Rev. Temple questioned sarcastically.

Josh McDaniel began reading thru the newspaper again mumbling and shaking.

"How could he?" said Josh McDaniel angrily. "What was he thinking when he printed this? How embarrassing? I must apologize to these people immediately."

Rev. Temple tried to calm Josh McDaniel and reassured him that they were doing everything they could to support Jessica Blandon and the mayor.

"Well good for Sherry that she resigned. I'm proud of her for taking a stand like that," Josh remarked while putting the newspapers down. "Make sure I give her a bonus for being the dedicated person she is. I'll certainly want her back on the staff."

Josh picked the newspapers back up and shook his head as he glanced thru them again. Laying the papers aside he frowned and continued to grumble as he started getting out of bed saying he had "to go to the office." Dollie quickly pushed him back down and worked to persuade him to remain in the hospital. Despite Josh's insistence he was finally convinced recovery was number one on the list for him.

"You have to stay here," commented Rev. Temple. "I'll keep you informed of everything, but you need to get well. It won't do any good if you have another heart attack or worse."

"But Jack, something has to be done now!" expressed Josh with anger in his voice.

"I have invited Barbara to talk to you and together I am

thinking we can put together a plan to get the public back on the mayor's side. They need to learn that in America a person is innocent until proven guilty."

"Well said Jack!" cheered Dollie as she had sat quietly until this moment.

"So what is the plan?" questioned Josh. "Sounds like you have been putting a lot of thought to this."

"I'll wait for Barbara as part of the plan is hers. We are not going to do anything until you approve it. It does involve the newspaper. We thought it was time to have an article about Lee on the front page of the next issue, but of course we need hard facts and more information than we have now."

"Exactly!" agreed Josh. "I don't want anything in that paper that can't be proven so get the facts. This time the watch dog will be on the job."

"And not foaming at the mouth as it has been the past sensationalized two weeks under the leadership of Lee," added Dollie Burgess.

In another half hour, Barbara Mayfield entered Josh's hospital room and the three of them went to work figuring out how to take on Lee Downs.

"We need facts and a lot of them. There is a lot of story not known by us and we need to know it all before printing anything in the newspaper," said Josh McDaniel.

Barbara Mayfield had brought information from the construction company including records to verify what had happened during the time her dad was president of the labor union. She also brought the file that the mayor had shown Rev. Temple earlier that day.

On the way to the hospital, Rev. Temple had made a quick stop at the coroner's office where he filled out the proper papers requesting a copy of the autopsy performed on Leonard Downwright. Rev. Temple was to pick it up later and was told a copy of the death certificate would be included.

Dollie Burgess saw the three were going to be involved for a while going thru the company files and folder so she quietly excused herself and rushed home to get a Tubberware container of cookies and thermos of lemonade to share with the investigating group. She wanted to do her part in cracking the mystery of Lee Downs and providing food and drink were her specialty.

On her way, Dollie spotted Jessica Blandon who was loading groceries she had bought at the market. Dollie pulled up beside Jessica and asked if she would care to go to the hospital to visit Josh McDaniel. She explained that Josh had just been given copies of the newspapers and was outraged and wanted to apologize to her.

Jessica quickly agreed to accompany Dollie as she knew Josh wasn't at fault about the articles. She wanted to assure Josh that she was fine and had gotten to where she and her family were laughing about the stories in the newspaper now.

CHAPTER ELEVEN

Dr. Boling pulled out the medical charts of Josh McDaniel and examined closely the vital signs of the past few hours. He looked at the blood pressure report and noted the heart monitor. After looking the chart over he commented that things were "looking pretty good."

The doctor took Josh's wrist and started to take the pulse, but stopped for a second to make an adjustment on the IV still dripping medications into Josh's system. The doctor's eyes then widened as he realized how fast Josh's heart was beating.

"Your heart is racing terribly fast. What happened?" asked Dr. Boling as he examined Josh's legs and arms. He looked into Josh's face and lifted one eyelid and then the other.

He looked puzzled as he began to share with Josh his concern about these sudden changes. He noted this increase speed by the heart was not good. The doctor turned toward the nurses and ordered them not to let Josh out of bed or to have company.

Josh nodded in the affirmative and expressed his

intention to follow orders. They shook hands in agreement as Dr. Boling turned to leave.

As the doctor exited the room, a custodian moving a table backed into Dr. Boling. The custodian quickly apologized and turned red with embarrassment. As soon as Dr. Boling had moved out of the doorway, the custodian moved the large table into Josh's room while a nurse plugged in a telephone and sat it on the table. Another nurse rolled a large blackboard on a stand into the room. Another sat two folding chairs in the corner.

Dr. Boling leaned back into the room with a raised eyebrow and looked at Josh.

"What is this?"

The nurse and orderly scurried out of the room and away from hearing distance.

"Is this what I prescribed?" asked Dr. Boling.

"Certainly," replied Josh McDaniel. "You said not to be stressed and if I don't start working on this problem that has come up I'll be plenty stressed."

The doctor rolled his eyes and looked at the nurses' station where the nurses seemed to give a slight shrug of their shoulders to show they had tried to get Josh to rest.

"Well," began Dr. Boling," if you must--please try not to move around too much and certainly rest. I'm giving orders to the nurses to check on your regularly to insure you are following orders."

Dr. Boling started to leave and then stepped back in the room and approached Josh. Staring straight at him with deep concern he said, "Josh, we need you in this community. You are a good man. You are constantly doing things to help people. I don't want you dying on me. Please listen to me. You have got to get rest and use restraint in getting involved in whatever it is you are about to be doing. Please promise me you will rest and go slow."

"Thanks Doc," Josh said as he picked up a folder and began reading it. "I'll rest and promise to do my best to go slow."

Hopelessly Dr. Boling took the folder out of Josh's hand and looked at him eye to eye. "Please Josh. Try to rest and don't get involved in some big project. We need you well."

Josh's eagerness to settle the situation quickly caused him to take charge of the investigation. He was determined to undo the mess that Lee Downs had brought on the community using Josh's newspaper. Somehow this matter was going to be settled. Before its conclusion Josh hoped the community would be aware of how important it is to check the facts and insure they are true.

"God did not put that commandment in the list of ten for nothing," he thought as he lay there preparing the battle. "'Thou shall not bear false witness against thy neighbor.'"

He paused for a moment to think about Lee. He hoped Lee was misled in his desire to sensationalize the news and that he was just doing what he thought was his job. Josh did not want to think that Lee was involved in some mysterious crime developing in Sassafras Springs. He liked the young man and hoped he would turn out to be a good journalist and not a person wanting vengeance toward the mayor.

Dollie arrived with cookies in hand which Josh promptly grabbed with great appreciation. When he looked up he saw Jessica Blandon. He immediately broke down offering her a sincere apology. Jessica reassured him everything was fine and although it was a rough time she knew he would never do anything like that to her. They shook hands and smiled.

Rev. Temple and Barbara Mayfield arrived from lunch and immediately everyone got to work on dividing the materials and categorizing them. The group listed everything they could think of concerning the articles, the people involved and the new information that had come to light. As they talked and exchanged information they began to organize and examine the facts about Lee Downwright and family. The group was surprised to see a remarkable connection between several of the people involved.

"So what do we have?" Josh asked. "Maybe it would help if we wrote everything on this blackboard so we can see it and move it around on the board as we organize it in different ways."

Dollie Burgess cleaned off the blackboard and promptly pulled it over to the table so it would be easy to reach. She wrote on the board what she heard them saying. On one side of the blackboard she put information and how everyone was connected. On the other side was a list of things that the group needed to verify as facts.

The blackboard was normally used by the nurses to write their work schedule and a list of the various patients and who was to be caring for each one. Dollie knew Jack and Josh would work together easier if everything was organized on a blackboard so she made arrangements with the nurses to borrow the blackboard for the day.

"We need to designate separately what we know as fact and what we assume or suspect. Let's put 'f' by those which are fact and 's' by those we suspect to make sure we don't start going off on wild ideas. That can get us in trouble," suggested Rev. Temple.

"First, we know that Mr. & Mrs. Winston Downwright, parents of Leonard Downwright, are to have lived here in Sassafras Springs according to the obituary here in the mayor's information. Does anyone know where? Does anyone know anything about them?" asked Rev. Temple.

"I never heard of them," volunteered Dollie Burgess. "Jessica, did you know any Downwrights in Sassafras Springs?"

"Afraid not," she answered.

"Write on the board Jackson Coleman and Millie (Coleman) Downwright," instructed Josh. "Do we know any other relatives?"

Jessica Blandon slowly raised her hand. She had a rather puzzled look on her face.

"It just occurred to me," began Jessica Blandon. "The mayor's wife gets her hair done at my beauty shop and one day she said her maiden name was really Coleman instead of Collins--that her family had to change it when she was young. Seems peculiar that Collins and Coleman would be connected with the mayor and these other people."

The whole group turned with widened eyes in surprise at this news provided by Jessica Blandon. After a moment of silence they reviewed everything with this new revelation from Jessica. They searched their minds trying to put it in to some kind of order.

"Very good point, Jessica," remarked Josh. "I think we need to check into several things. We still have not found a couple named Downwright in the community. There must be something at the county clerk's office. Might check for property owned by the Downwrights."

"I'll go to the city clerk's office now as it may take a while to track down that information and on the way back I can stop by and pick up the coroner's report," said Rev. Temple. "Now let me get this straight. There should be a property owned by the Downwrights in Sassafras Springs? Correct?"

"Not if they rented," pointed out Dollie Burgess.

"Oh, that would be true. Good thinking Dollie," commented Rev. Temple. "So what do we do if they didn't own land?"

"How about phone books? The Historical Society has a collection of past phonebooks. There might be a phone number in one of them for the Downwrights," suggested Jessica Blandon.

"Good work, Jessica," applauded Josh McDaniel as Dollie Burgess patted Jessica Blandon on the back with praise for another good idea. "That might be our only way to track them down. Jack, go ahead and go to the clerk's office to get information on the Downwrights owning land and Jessica, you go to the research center of the Historical Society and check the phonebooks. Also while you are there check the cemetery records and obituary records for Coleman, Collins and Downwright. Let's see who else could be involved? You might include a look at Wallingford too. That Collins and Coleman connection bothers me."

"What should I do, Josh?" asked Dollie Burgess.

"You stay with me right now, but Barbara," began Josh, "time for you to go to work at the newspaper. There are filing cabinets in the front section of the business. They include obituaries and information on nearly everyone in the area. Every article that has been included in the newspapers about a certain family is clipped and added to the folder. Check for Coleman, Collins and Downwright information. Yes, you better check Wallingford. I know that is your family and we are working to support your father, but we have to leave no stone unturned. Copy and bring back here as quickly as you can. Tell Lee you are researching an article you are preparing and will show him the story at the end of the day. He won't have anything for you to type today but tomorrow you will be very busy. We need you there to let us know what he is doing."

"This is rather fun," laughed Barbara Mayfield. "Had no idea the newspaper business would be this exciting. I would have gone to work there a long time ago."

"Hummm," frowned Josh McDaniel. "Don't get too

cute and signal Lee we are doing this. We must keep it totally quiet."

Barbara, Jack, and Jessica disappeared on their search for additional information. Dollie and Josh went to work writing the information on the blackboard. They listed all the involved characters they knew at this point and left a place to write how they were connected. At this point, the obituary for Leonard Downwright was the only information that actually connected the people. That alone was not reliable enough to make accusations or to print conclusions in the newspaper.

"Josh," began Dollie Burgess, "the mayor's wife was a Collins. Isn't that what Jessica said?"

"Yes, she seemed to think that Mollie had said that while getting her hair fixed one day. If that was true, does that mean she could be a sister to Jackson Coleman? Surely the mayor would have known that."

"Wait a minute!" Dollie exclaimed.

"What? What do you have?" asked Josh.

"Millie Downwright and Mollie would both have the last name Coleman. That would make them Millie and Mollie Coleman. Do they sound like twins perhaps? Ok, ok, ok. I'm jumping to conclusions that nothing has provided information for."

"Actually, that thought occurred to me too. The only thing that bothers me is the idea that the mayor surely would know that his wife was a twin. He would surely know that Jackson Coleman was his brother-in-law. How could the mayor not be aware of these things?"

A few hours later the group reassembled in the hospital room and went to work adding their findings to the blackboard. Rev. Temple was first to return with the death certificate and the coroner's report.

"As far as the evidence shows Leonard Downwright was killed instantly when he hit the pavement from a six story fall from a building being built downtown," reported Rev. Temple. "The only question that the coroner had was why Leonard was on the sixth floor when earlier in the day he had requested to go home because of feeling dizzy. According to the report he had left four hours earlier and by the time he was back on the sixth floor the crew had left for the day. The boss had ended work for the crew two hours earlier than usual."

Josh McDaniel and Dollie Burgess nodded at each other as they realized that something was not quite right with the report. They all agreed that Leonard Downwright might have been murdered, but labeled it with an "s" for suspected idea rather than an "f" for fact.

As Rev. Temple finished Jessica Blandon arrived with a phone number that revealed that the house where Mr. and Mrs. Winston Downwright lived was where the Mayor and Mrs. Wallingford now live.

"I don't believe it," remarked Josh McDaniel. "The mayor is right in the middle of everything. How can he not know what is going on?"

Jessica Blandon reported when she checked the obituary files at the historical society's research center that the folders on the Collins family and Coleman family were empty; the Downwright folder had only the same obituary they already had; and the Wallingford folder included only the parents of the mayor and their ancestors. She said she asked the research assistant about it and he said that the folders according to their checkout register had been examined by a Roger Coleman the day before. She was surprised to find that everything in the folders was missing.

"Coleman?" remarked Dollie Burgess. "Did you say Roger Coleman?"

"Yes," replied Jessica Blandon. "I immediately checked the guest register to see if he had signed it and if he listed an address."

"Well?" the entire group questioned together.

"He did and he wrote he was from Arnold, Missouri," she answered.

"Arnold," laughed Josh McDaniel. "That's where my family was from. We moved here---?"

"Arnold?" interrupted Rev. Temple. "The mayor told me today that is where he met his wife and they were married about a week later. The date was within a week of the death of Leonard Downwright."

"What's wrong Josh," asked Dollie Burgess. "You look like you have seen a ghost."

"Never mind," Josh McDaniel said quickly. "Put a note on the blackboard about the empty folders."

Despite the lack of information, the missing folders seemed significant enough to make a notation on the blackboard. As they finished adding this information Rev. Temple's cell phone rang. It was Barbara Mayfield.

"He is what?" asked Rev. Temple. "Coming here? Now? But---got it. Thanks Barbara. Get here when you can. No, better yet, I'll meet you at Porter's Place and we can go thru the folders if there is much in them. You say they are all four rather thick. Good---surely we'll find something in them that will help."

Josh McDaniel and Dollie Burgess knew immediately that Lee Downwright was on his way so they started picking up things and putting them out of sight. Dollie and Jessica Blandon rolled the blackboard out of the room and around the corner placing a sheet over it to conceal the writing on it. Dollie took a seat next to Josh who was back laying flat on the bed like he was too weak to visit.

"Jessica," began Rev. Temple. "You better go with me.

You have done a great job so far. You may have some other ideas as we go through the materials and it will be better if you aren't seen by Lee. We don't want him getting any ideas."

"Sure thing," she replied. "Mind if we catch a bite to eat while there? I didn't have lunch and I could sure use one of Ike's specialties."

As soon as the others had left the room Dollie turned to Josh and said, "Ok, Mr. McDaniel, I know that look on your face. So what scared you earlier?"

"Nothing Dollie," he replied. "It just reminded me of when my parents and I moved to Sassafras Springs. We were hardly here two months and the car exploded and killed dad. Remember?"

"I remember," said Dollie with a trembling voice. "I remember it very well. We were both standing there in the yard when it happened. I'll never forget that day."

"Mom took it rather hard too," said Josh. "Well, why wouldn't she. The man she loved had been blown up. I was devastated but I know it must have hurt her more. She just gave up on life that day. It wasn't a year before she died. I always said it was a broken heart."

Dollie patted him on the back.

The two of them fell quiet as their hands met and grasped each other. The memory of that day when two young 13 year olds were forced to grow up a little faster than most once again shook them. The blast. The flames. The flying debris. It was all too vivid in their memories. It seemed like it had just happened.

"Is this a bad time?" said Lee as he entered the room with a bouquet of carnations from the florist shop. "You look pretty depressed. I hope everything is alright."

"Oh yes," laughed Josh as he tried to change the mood.

"We were remembering something that happened a long time ago."

"Well," began Lee, "tell me how you are doing. You already seem a little better than you looked when I came in. Say, I see you have copies of the newspapers. What did you think?"

"I think we need to talk," replied Josh in a calm quiet voice.

"The circulation nearly doubled by the second newspaper," proudly said Lee. "We all worked together to put out a good looking and interesting newspaper for you Josh. The people were fighting to get copies at Ike's by the second issue."

Josh was hesitant to say anything. Dollie immediately interrupted with the offer of a cookie from the Tupperware container and asked if he would like some fresh lemonade. Josh smiled and nodded at her pleasant and helpful way of changing the subject. Dollie had come to the rescue again.

CHAPTER TWELVE

"Barbara," began Rev. Temple, "you weren't kidding about these folders. My word, there is a lot of material here. It will take us a week."

Ike Winston approached them with menus and poured coffee for all of them. They motioned thank you and pointed at the "special of the day" sign to let him know they wanted the special---a tuna fish and apple salad sandwich. Without a word they were sorting thru the Coleman file and passing the articles around.

Ike quickly returned and took a quick glance over the stack of folders and articles and started to speak but realized they were too involved to stop for him. He set a plate of sweet rolls down and napkins and left.

Barbara Mayfield laughed as she opened the first newspaper clipping from the Coleman folder. Here was success immediately. It was the birth announcement for triplets being born. The three girls were named Molina, Melissa and Millicent.

The three of them stopped and looked at each other.

"Three?" their lips said together without making a sound. "They were triplets?"

"Molina would be Mollie I am guessing. There is Millie who would be this Millicent listed, but who is Melissa?" asked Rev. Temple.

"Mollie is Mrs. Wallingford and Millie is Mrs. Downwright. Then there is one more…..another piece of the puzzle to be found," laughed Jessica Blandon who was beginning to enjoy the mystery as it unfolded with new information hourly.

She took a sweet roll and bit into it responding with an expression of how delicious it was. She took the plate of rolls and handed it to Barbara Mayfield.

"Here, try this," she said.

One more time they reread the article then shuffled thru the other articles to find more information about the three sisters. The date on the article did fit the age of Mrs. Wallingford, the mayor's wife, but that wouldn't prove anything conclusively. They needed something better. After picking up the articles carefully one by one they soon realized there were no other articles about the triplets or the three women. They did find Downwright's obituary which seemed strange since this was the Coleman file.

"Maybe there is something about the triplets in the Collins folder because of the change of name from Coleman to Collins," suggested Jessica.

"Good thinking Jessica," responded Rev. Temple.

"I can't believe my mother was this Mollie Coleman," questioned Barbara Mayfield. "Why wouldn't I know that she was a triplet? It doesn't make sense to me."

"A lot of things in this case don't make sense," added Rev. Temple.

They took the Collins folder and began searching for information on the triplets. There was nothing in it except the Leonard Downwright obituary that kept surfacing every place they looked and a couple of articles about Mrs. Wallingford's parents, Mr. and Mrs. Riley Collins.

"I think we are at a dead end with these folders or are we missing something?" questioned Rev. Temple.

The three of them gathered the information from the Coleman file and placed it aside. The Collins file was sorted thru again without any new evidence and finally set aside. They took the Wallingford file and began taking one article at a time. Since Rick Wallingford was mayor there were a number of articles about his campaign and his service to the community. There were also a number of articles featuring Mrs. Wallingford as she had served as president of the local Bridge Club and also the Women's Study Club. There was even a picture of Barbara being crowned homecoming queen.

"Nothing here," began Rev. Temple, "but may I say you were a ravishing homecoming queen?"

"Wait," interrupted Barbara Mayfield. "I may have something. Didn't we read an article about Mr. & Mrs. Riley Collins being my mom's parents in the Collins folder? Those are my grandparents. I don't ever remember meeting them as they died about the time I was born, but surely that releases mom from being involved with this group."

"Yes, but maybe no," exclaimed Rev. Temple. "The question is, 'Are those really Mollie's parents?' If so were they originally Mr. and Mrs. Coleman or someone completely different?"

"I'm so confused," sighed Jessica Blandon.

Rev. Temple and Jessica Blandon took bites from their sweet rolls they had started to eat, took a sip of coffee and turned their attention on Barbara Mayfield when they saw her eyes get big. They leaned forward to see the article Barbara was reading. Barbara was nodding and mumbling.

Her expression revealed she had something that had surprised her.

"What is it?" Rev. Temple asked.

"This mentions that Mr. and Mrs. Jack Coleman, Mr. & Mrs. Winston Downwright and Mrs. Rick Wallingford were all at the same party."

"Well, that doesn't seem too unusual. They all knew each other," commented Rev. Temple.

"It says the Colemans and Downwrights lived in Arnold and Mrs. Wallingford in O'Fallon," Barbara Mayfield continued.

"And----," said Rev. Temple expecting to hear more information.

"Yes, but they were all at the home of Mr. and Mrs. Jasper McDaniel here in Sassafras Springs. It says the McDaniels had recently moved here."

"That name sounds familiar," questioned Jessica Blandon. "Who is that? Where have I heard that name?"

"They were Josh's parents! We now have a connection between the Downwrights and Josh McDaniel. Ok...this is getting ridiculous."

"I'm sorry," meekly said Jessica Blandon. "I am lost."

"At the home of Mr. and Mrs. Jasper McDaniel.," Barbara Mayfield repeated with a tone of amazement.

"Ok," commented Jessica Blandon. "So, what is the point? We know they all knew each other."

"Mr. and Mrs. Jasper McDaniel are Josh McDaniel's parents. Did you get that? But I didn't tell you one other statement in the article. The reason they were having the party at the McDaniel's home was the occasion of the women's birthday celebration."

"Josh's mother is Melissa?" shouted Rev. Temple. "Impossible! Surely he would know that."

"Not necessarily," began Barbara Mayfield. "His father

was killed in a terrible car explosion a week later after this party according to the date on this clipping. They had just moved here from Arnold. Mrs. McDaniel went into a state of depression. I can remember my mother worrying about her and she would go over to visit frequently. Mrs. McDaniel died about a year later of depression and Josh was sent to California to live with his grandparents. He was only around 13 at the time. I was 4 and idolized him. I remember my mom explaining why he had left. I certainly was unaware that we were related to any of these people though it did seem like the McDaniels were at our house or we were over there a lot. At that young age I don't think I would have remembered them at all if it wasn't that they came so often. Hummm. Strange, but it seems to fit now."

There was a hush that came over the group.

Finally Barbara Mayfield interrupted the silence. "Well, that explains why mom was so worried about Mrs. McDaniel. They were sisters. Wonder why Dad wasn't at the party?"

"Yeah!" responded Jessica Blandon.

The three of them sat there for a while contemplating everything they had found. Now they knew who the triplets were and that possibly two of their husbands had been killed within a week of the birthday celebration.

"So if they were somehow intending to keep it secret that they were related or that they had changed their name from Coleman to Collins why did this appear in the newspaper?" asked Jessica Blandon.

"Good point Jessica," replied Rev. Temple. "I suspect it was not intended for the newspaper and that may have been the reason the two men were killed."

"Now wait," interrupted Barbara Mayfield. "We don't know they were killed and we are talking about my family."

They all three took another bite from their sweet rolls and a sip of coffee then looked at each other with a puzzled look.

"So Josh is my cousin," said Barbara Mayfield out loud. "Well, that certainly is a twist."

"So how do we tell Josh? Or what do we tell Josh?" asked Rev. Temple.

Barbara shrugged her shoulders. "I feel like I'm dreaming. None of this can be true. It is like everything I thought was real isn't any more."

"Let's go to the count records department and try to get birth, marriage and death certificates for all of these. That should help put things in perspective," suggested Rev. Temple.

Lee Downs visited with Josh McDaniel and Dollie Burgess for over an hour and Dollie had given some hints to Lee that it was time for him to go. Yet she hesitated to straight out say for him to leave. It was apparent that Lee was concerned about something and had something he wanted to say to Josh.

"Maybe he feels guilty for the articles and wants to tell Josh about them," Dollie thought with hope that maybe Lee wasn't all bad.

"Josh," began Lee, "Forgive me but I was looking for some forms for the mailing to our out of town subscribers and was going thru your desk drawers when I found these pictures. Would you mind telling me who they are?"

Josh became pale. Dollie leaned over and gasped. Memories started rolling rapidly back for both of them as they remembered the explosion.

"These are my parents," replied Josh with emotion in his voice.

"These are your parents?" responded Lee blinking his eyes in disbelief. "I don't understand. My mother had these pictures in an album she kept in the trunk upstairs at our house. Why would she have your parents' pictures?"

Josh McDaniel looked surprised at Lee Downs.

"I don't have a clue," Josh finally replied after taking a deep breath.

"I was really confused when I found them. So much so I went back to my apartment and got the album. Here it is. There are other pictures of them in the album. I thought you might like to see them."

Josh took the album struggling to hold it with the IV in his wrist. Dollie helped him as he opened the first page. He didn't recognize anyone. He turned the page and to his surprise there was his father and mother in wedding attire.

"Where did you get these?" ordered Josh who was becoming very uneasy. "What kind of trick are you trying to pull? Look! My father died in an explosion when I was 13. I was standing right there when the car blew up. So was Dollie. It was awful!"

"Lee," interrupted Dollie, "are you trying to push Josh to have another heart attack? What kind of game are you playing? Get out of her right now!"

Dollie stood and started yanking on Lee's arm to drag him out. She was shouting for someone to come help her. Lee stood his ground and begged her to stop.

"Look," began Lee Downs, "I don't know what is going on here. I just found these pictures and my pictures are the same plus some others. They are other relatives I think."

Lee broke down and cried. He was shaking all over.

"Seriously, I was as surprised as anyone when I saw the pictures in Josh's desk this morning," explained Lee.

Josh turned the page and to his surprise looked at a picture of himself with his parents. He grabbed Dollie's arm and pulled her away from Lee. He pointed to the picture. Dollie gasped as she pointed to another. There she and Josh were as teenagers arm in arm laughing and swinging in the front porch swing.

Lee watched the two long time friends struggle with memories of a time when they were young lovers. They turned the page and found yet another one of them with Josh holding a baby.

"I remember holding that baby," laughed Josh. "I was holding it the day of mom's funeral. I even remember them saying it was a week old. I don't remember who it was but some young girl had come by and mom remarked that the baby boy was my cousin. She hoped someday I would get to know him better."

"That's me," said Lee weakly.

"You?" said Dollie and Josh as they jerked their heads up to look at Lee and then back down to compare the features.

"By golly, I think it could be you," said a surprised Josh McDaniel.

"My father died in a construction site. They said he fell off a six story building or killed himself, but I don't believe it. I never knew him as I was born two months later in January."

"Who was your dad?" questioned Josh McDaniel.

"Leonard Downwright," replied Lee.

"My mother died in January two months after Leonard Downwright died, " responded Josh McDaniel as he started sorting thru memories. "Your dad was Leonard Downwright? I can't believe it. I had forgotten about the Downwright story. I remember dad and mom talking about it and I could tell they were deeply worried about it."

"I was eventually placed in a foster home and they shortened my name to Downs," explained Lee. "They said

I had to forget I was a Downwright and to not tell anyone. I never did understand."

Josh shared how he remembered Lee's mother struggling as a young widow and after a very difficult year placed Lee in a foster home and disappeared. It all fit together.

"Actually, she didn't completely disappear. It was a strange relationship we had while I was growing up," commented Lee Downs. "When I got to be a teenager she would show up at the house usually at the back door and visit for a few minutes and then disappear. She never explained why we couldn't be together or where she was the rest of the time. I was totally confused."

Lee went on to explain how he had thought for years that Mayor Wallingford had been involved in killing his father, Leonard Downwright, Sr. until he visited him earlier in the week. Lee shared how he had been determined to get the mayor to admit killing Leonard Downright.

"Then I was about to leave," added Lee, "and looked up and there was Mrs. Wallingford's picture above the fireplace. Turn the page in the photo album. There it is. The same picture. I was stunned."

There was no doubt. The picture was Mollie Wallingford--the same person that was hanging above the fireplace at the Wallingford house. Lee asked why she would be in this same album with Josh's parents and his parents since she was a Collins. He was very confused at all of this and was hoping Josh could explain some things to him.

"I'm sorry Lee," Josh began, "I was in California with my grandparents after mom died. I'm just as shocked at all of this as you are. I have no idea"

"So you really didn't know your parents very long?" Lee asked.

"That's right," Josh continued. "My mother went into such a state of depression after Dad was blown up in the car explosion that she died of a broken heart--at least that is what I always thought. It was a heart attack I found when I started doing some research on my own. If it had not been for Mollie Wallingford coming regularly to visit and helping out I don't know what I would have done."

"That's right!" exclaimed Dollie. "I remember her being there many times when I would come over to see you. It never occurred to me at the time, but why would she be there? How did she get to know your mother as she lived clear on the other side of town? She brought food often didn't she? I can even remember little Barbara bringing banana muffins. Remember?"

"They have a daughter?" asked Lee.

"Ah! Yes," said Dollie as she remembered they wanted to keep Barbara's identity a secret. "She has been living away from here for a long time."

"What?" remarked Josh as Dollie winked and nodded to remind Josh not to tell that Barbara was the daughter of the mayor, "Oh yes, she was living back east I think."

"My mother is still alive but I don't get to see her. She calls once in a while but insists it is better I don't know where she is," whined Lee. "I don't understand why she can't be here with me or I can't go see her. Do you suppose she is in prison or something? It has been that way nearly all my life. She keeps saying everything is alright and that one day we'll be together. I don't understand any of this. Then in the foster home I was forced to use the name of the family taking care of me. It was Collins."

"Forced to use their name?" questioned Dollie. "I never heard of such a thing."

"They said it was to protect me," he laughed. "Can you imagine anything so silly? I wanted to be me so I changed my name back to the shortened Downs instead of Downwright as soon as I graduated from high school."

Josh and Dollie looked at each other. They had a lot of questions and didn't know where to begin. Then there was the matter of whether to trust Lee and open up and start talking to him. Dollie and Josh glanced back and forth as the conversation went on and finally Josh whispered to Dollie that they had better wait and find out more before opening up to Lee.

"I hope Jack and the girls can find some additional information that will shed light on this confused mess," commented Dollie in private to Josh.

"Lee," began Josh, "these pictures have taken me back years with memories. Do you think I could look at them closer overnight? I promise to get them back to you."

"I don't know," Lee said picking them up and holding them close to his chest. "That's all I have of my parents now. Everything else was sold or thrown away. I do have the trunk that the pictures were in."

"Please," pressed Josh, "I won't lose them here in the hospital and it will give me something to look at. Maybe it will bring a memory back that will enable me to help explain things."

"Well, if you think you might remember something. I guess it would be worth a try. Please take care of it though. Don't let anyone touch the album," requested Lee Downs.

Lee insisted he would be back to get them the next day. He also stressed he needed to get back to the newspaper to make sure it was ready for printing tomorrow.

After Lee was gone Dollie took the album. She slowly turned the pages and nodded her head remembering the various people and wondering why Lee would have the pictures. Just as she finished she heard voices coming down the hall.

"Sounds like Jack coming and he sounds wound up. They must have found something," said Josh.

At that moment the trio bounced around the corner and into the hospital room. They smiled and obviously were excited about something. Dollie closed the album and carefully laid it aside. Josh sat back up and adjusted his IV to prepare to hear what they had to say. Jessica Blandon pulled the blackboard back in the room and carefully removed the sheet that was covering it. Rev. Temple and Barbara Mayfield pulled chairs closer.

"Josh," laughed Barbara Mayfield. "We are cousins. Your mother and my mother are sisters and their sister was Mrs. Downwright. We are all related. Mollie, Millie and Melissa are triplets. We found a clipping announcing their birth and although I find it hard to believe that you and I did not know this all these years it is true."

After the shock wore off Josh opened the photo album and revealed the pictures that Lee had brought. He announced to the group that the young man's real name was Lee Downwright, Jr. He shared what Lee reported and the group then turned to the blackboard to begin piecing everything together.

They wrote the names of the three sisters as Rev. Temple reported the findings. "There was Melissa Coleman who was born in 1943. She married Jasper McDaniel who was killed in a car explosion in 1979 a few months after the couple and their son---that's you Josh---had moved from Arnold to Sassafras Springs. The couple hosted Mrs. Rick Wallingford of O'Fallon, Mr. & Mrs. Winston Downwright, Mr. and Mrs. Leonard Downwright and Mr. & Mrs. Jackson Coleman, all of Arnold, for a birthday party for the triplets a few weeks before Jasper was killed."

Josh then added, "For the record, I married Rachel Binder in 1985. She was killed in a gas explosion at a hotel in Los Angeles on our honeymoon. At the time it was thought that everyone in the building was killed including me. I had gone to the real estate office to check on a surprise I had planned for my wife---a condo in Modesto."

"Molina (Mollie) Coleman was born in 1943," began Rev. Temple again. "Her parents were Mr. & Mrs. Riley Collins. The parents were both killed in a car accident in 1978 or they probably would have been at the birthday party too."

"Rick Wallingford met Mollie at the home of Mr. & Mrs. Jackson Coleman and started dating her and at this point in time she was using the last name Collins like her parents. Rick and Mollie were married in 1974 and had Barbara, their daughter, in 1975. Barbara married Jacob Mayfield who was later killed in Iraq while working with contractors there."

"We know these things are true because we have the newspaper clippings to back it up except the information you just gave us," reported Barbara Mayfield.

"Afraid that won't hold up," commented Josh. "Remember the newspapers don't always tell the truth as we have seen in recent weeks here in Sassafras Springs. I remember the articles in the newspapers about the explosion. I was grief stricken at the loss of my wife. Otherwise I would have been questioning the newspapers to understand what had happened. In the newspapers they said there was evidence that it was deliberately set."

"Did you say deliberately set?" gasped Barbara. "Did you ever find what happened?"

"No," quietly responded Josh McDaniel. "Now we need some things to back up what the newspaper said."

"We went to the computer and tried to get the birth certificates," began Rev. Temple.

"Good work!" shouted Josh McDaniel. "That's the way to do it!"

"Surprisingly the entire network at the bureau was

down," replied Rev. Temple. "They were not able to get anything on the computer the entire time we were there. They said they would send us the information we requested as soon as the computers were back online."

The name of Millicent (Millie) Coleman's name was placed on the blackboard.

"She was born in 1943 and married Winston Downwright in 1958 at the age of 15. The very young couple gave birth to Leonard Downwright Sr. a couple of months later in 1958. Leonard died in 1978 when he was pushed off a six story building or fell off. His son, Leonard Downwright, Jr. was born a couple of months later in January, 1979. The mother disappeared for a couple of years and the baby was taken by grandparents Mollie & Winston Downwright who were living in Sassafras Springs in the house where the Mayor now lives. The couple and grandson Leonard Downwright were in a car accident in 1979 when a tractor trailer which tried to pass them edged them off the road on the side of a mountain in Colorado. Remarkably the baby Leonard Downwright Jr. survived and was placed in a foster home. The grandparents were burned in the car explosion."

"Lee said he was forced to go by the name of the family he lived with," commented Josh McDaniel. "Did you find out what their name was?"

"Yes," began Barbara. "It was Riley Collins."

"I must not have heard you," responded Josh McDaniel.

"Riley Collins," repeated Barbara.

"Isn't that your grandparents?" asked Josh McDaniel.

"I am getting terribly confused," laughed Barbara. "You are right. So Lee actually lived with my---er, ah, his grandparents who had changed their name from Coleman to Collins."

Dollie Burgess got up and began pacing back and

forth looking at the information on the blackboard. She would point to one and carry her finger across the board to another name. She then turned to the group and shrugged her shoulders.

There was silence as they all stared at the blackboard. Their eyes went back and forth over the materials. Frequent sighs were heard as they struggled to make sense of it all.

"Barbara," began Josh, "it is time you brought your parents here. We need to hear what they know and can verify for sure. We don't have enough to make decisions."

"How can you say that," broke in Barbara. "Look at it! Our mothers were sisters and Lee's grandmother was another sister."

"But why did we not know this," persisted Josh McDaniel.

"Good point," Rev. Temple added in a supportive manner. "There are a lot of things here which though they appear to be connected are too strange. There has to be something we are missing."

Barbara left to get her parents. Rev. Temple called the church to let the board know he would not be able to be at the board meeting as he was working with Josh on a serious matter. Dollie slipped away to prepare some sandwiches and raspberry tea for the group to enjoy when they got hungry.

CHAPTER THIRTEEN

The next morning Lee was delivering newspapers and selling a huge number as the public was eager to find out what sensational things had happened in their community since the last issue.

Headlines proclaimed, "MAYOR RE-EXAMINED FOR EMBEZZLEMENT OF UNION FUNDS." The article claimed the Missouri Attorney General was coming to Sassafras Springs to bail out Mayor Wallingford while on the campaign trail for Governor. The article claimed that Attorney General Randall Coleman was a nephew of the mayor.

The article continued explaining how the newspaper editor Josh McDaniel had been related to the mayor and covered up the truth about the government's illegal dealings and how the mayor was pulling the same financial scheme he had done with the union. The article went on to suggest that Mayor Wallingford had repeated the same fraudulent scheme while in O'Fallon as a member of the city council.

"Lee," began Ike Winston, proprietor of Porter's Place, "I'm not sure I want you distributing your newspapers in my business any more. Our newspaper had a reputation of being fair and determined to print the truth, but since you took over it is nothing more than a supermarket tabloid. You can't tell me that Josh approves these articles you have been fabricating in the newspapers."

"Ike," replied Lee Downwright, "I'm hurt. This is the truth. I wouldn't print lies."

"Ike's right, you know," said Bill Owens of Owen's Electric and president of the school board. "Nothing you have printed since you took over has been straight truth. All you want to do is make money."

"Right," seconded Lincoln Madison, custodian of the school.

"Amen, brothers!" shouted Joan Stacy, choir director at the Nickerson Street Church as she sat her coffee cup down on the table. "I have wanted to say that since the first issue. You, Lee, are the devil!"

"People," began Lee Downwright, "I have the proof that Josh's mother and Mayor Wallingford's wife are sisters. There brother is the Attorney General's father. How much closer do you want to get for political schemes? Don't blame me for telling the truth. These people have been robbing you for nearly a dozen years."

"No, they haven't," said Margaret Cushing. "We know Josh and Mayor Wallingford and we know they are good decent people. They would never do what you are saying here."

Lee gathered his things and left Porter's Place. He had sold all the newspapers and was counting in his mind how many he needed to sell at the next business to break the record for sales in a week.

Meanwhile at the hospital the detective group was already at work trying to verify information as accurate or false. Mayor Wallingford and his wife joined them. When the blackboard was rolled in and uncovered the Mayor looked it over with a puzzled expression on his face.

"So what do you have here," questioned the Mayor. "What is all this? I don't understand."

Mrs. Wallingford was looking pale. She began to be a little weak in the knees and Dollie quickly helped her to the comfortable chair in the corner.

"Dear," began Mayor Wallingford in an excited voice as he went to his wife's side to help her. "Are you alright?"

"Oh my," she said as she went down on the chair. "How did you get all that information? You don't know what you have done."

"Dear?" said Mayor Wallingford as he kept shifting his eyes from her to the blackboard. "You know something about what they have there? What is it?"

Josh began by explaining to Mayor Wallingford what they had found. Mayor Wallingford laughed in a deep voice and shook his head.

"That can't be true," he said as he looked at his wife with a twinkle in his eyes convinced that they were playing a joke on him. "Do you have a camera to catch me looking funny?"

The mayor laughed until he saw that everyone else was very serious. He looked at his wife again hoping to find a smile or to cause her to break out in a laugh.

The group turned their attention to Mrs. Wallingford. She continued to look pale and weak. She had a very tense expression on her face. She was shaking. Mayor Wallingford went to her side and tenderly took her hand.

"Mollie?" he began, "Mollie what is going on? You do know something."

"My love," she began. "I don't know where to begin. It was so many years ago and so much has happened."

The group stood staring in silence. They didn't know

what to say. Dollie finally took a damp cold cloth to Mrs. Wallingford and wiped her face and gave her a smile and a pat on the back.

"Mollie," began Josh, "are you my aunt?"

Mayor Wallingford's mouth dropped open as he turned and looked stunned at Josh. He jerked his head back to Mollie when she nodded in the affirmative.

"Aunt?" questioned Mayor Wallingford. "Josh's aunt? I don't understand."

"Remember how I kept taking food to the McDaniel's when they lived here when Josh was a teenager?" she asked.

"Not really," he quietly responded.

"I remember, Mollie," began Dollie. "I remember you bringing Barbara and she would carry those delicious muffins to us. They were sure good. Josh remembers too. We talked about it."

Josh nodded in agreement as Mayor Wallingford began to speak, "Yes, I do remember now. I wondered about that then. I thought you must be the most caring person in the world to drive clear across town to take food to the McDaniels. Guess this would explain why."

Mayor Wallingford gave his wife a hug and then pushed her back slightly and asked, "You were sisters? Is that the situation? I don't know what to think now."

Mollie straightened up in the chair and began to get some color in her face. She looked at the blackboard and began to make a few corrections but generally approved everything on it. She looked at her husband.

"My love," she said as she put her arms around him as she got up from the chair. Then she backed up and said, "I have to tell you some things you don't know and that are not on the blackboard. My name is Mollie Coleman. I was Jackson Coleman's sister as is Josh's mother."

"Mollie and Melissa?" puzzled Mayor Wallingford. "You two weren't twins were you?"

"Not exactly," she began to answer as the others chuckled. He looked at them with a strange look wondering why they were laughing. "I'm one of a set of triplets."

Mayor Wallingford's mouth dropped open. He looked at the board and spotted the Downwright name. He pointed to it and they all nodded.

"You mean that upstart that is trying to drag me down is my nephew?"

"Yep," everyone replied.

"I don't understand."

"We are not sure about all of this either," replied Josh. "He was here and showed me this photo album. The whole family is in it including him as a baby in my arms. It was at mom's funeral."

"I remember that baby," smiled Mayor Wallingford as he took a look at the picture of Lee and his mother. "We really liked his mother. She was awfully young to have a child but she was a caring person. She wasn't your sister---no, that can't be right. She would be too young."

"Right," interrupted Mollie Wallingford. "Her husband was the son of my sister, Millie who married Winston Downwright. Their son was Leonard Downwright that worked with you in Arnold. He was the one who was pushed off the sixth floor in that building that was being built."

"We don't know if he was killed," corrected Mayor Wallingford.

"Yes we do," continued Mollie Wallingford. "Trust me. He was killed."

"But how can you be sure?" questioned Mayor Wallingford.

"Trust me," she said trying not to say anything more.

Josh then took over telling Mollie that it was time

that she shared everything. He explained how the lives of all of them were in danger and not knowing the truth or understanding what they were up against would be very dangerous. Mollie looked at them, cleared her throat and got very serious.

"Honey?" said Mayor Wallingford as he took his wife's hand and squeezed it. "Is there more we should know?"

She nodded her head and took a deep breath. She looked at Josh and lowered her head. She turned away and then got up and walked to the window that looked across the parking lot. As she stood there she saw someone roll out from under their car.

"NO!" she screamed. "Someone just put a bomb underneath our car."

The entire group ran to the window in time to see a man running to a waiting car which he jumped in. The car quickly disappeared out the parking lot exit. Mayor Wallingford stepped back and looked at his wife.

"Just what are we involved in Dear?"

"For the past 50 years the FBI has been protecting our family from the mob."

Everyone in the room got pale and tried to find a place to sit down. They looked at Mollie to see if she was serious. As they looked at her they could tell she was very serious. Rev. Temple took Mayor Wallingford's and Mollie's hands and bowed his head and prayed.

Dear Lord, we find ourselves overwhelmed with news and terrified of what the consequences could be. Please precious Lord, protect us all and help us to find a solution to the problems that are surrounding us. Help us to find peace, safety and strength in your watchful care. In your son's name we pray, Amen.

Rev. Temple reached for his cell phone and called the police to report the bomb. A few minutes later the parking lot was full of police and newsmen. The mayor and his wife were slipped out the back way and taken to a secret location. Josh was given 24 hour security by the local police department. Dollie remained there by his side choosing not to go out on the streets alone. Rev. Temple headed to the newspaper to pick up Barbara and to explain what had happened. He hoped to locate Lee and to deduce which side he was on.

At the newspaper office Rev. Temple found a line of people demonstrating against the mayor and Josh. The people were calling both Josh and the mayor robbers from the poor and asking for justice. The people were marching back and forth in front of the newspaper office chanting "Death to Men Like That."

Rev. Temple asked the demonstrators if they had seen Barbara and one demonstrator said Barbara had locked the office and left a few minutes earlier. The demonstrators had no idea where she was headed. When asked where Lee was they pointed to the courthouse.

Rev. Temple suddenly remembered that State Attorney Randall Coleman was expected to speak at the courthouse at noon. With the Mayor unable to attend it would be an embarrassment to the city for this state figure to be snubbed by the local government. Rev. Temple drove to the location where the speech was to be made and approached the political leader explaining that the mayor was unable to attend due to an emergency that had developed.

As he stood there a wadded newspaper was thrown at them. Rev. Temple picked it up as it unfolded to reveal the headlines. Rev. Temple stood in shock at the article. The state attorney looked over his shoulder and was shaken.

"I don't understand," the politician said. "What is all this?"

"I don't know for sure," said Rev. Temple hurriedly, "but we better get you out of here. This can't be a safe place to be."

CHAPTER FOURTEEN

"Hello," spoke Josh McDaniel into his cell phone. "Jack? Is that you? Good! I need to get out of the hospital. I have to get to the newspaper office and put out a newspaper."

"You know you aren't well enough and the crowds at your office are demonstrating against you and the mayor. It would be dangerous," responded Rev. Temple. "Besides, we don't know who else is out there looking for you. We know something is going on and you had better stay in the hospital with the police protection."

"I'm thinking if I put the whole story of our family in the newspaper," began Josh McDaniel, "it will straighten out this whole mess."

"Or get you all killed," warned Rev. Temple. "We have to work carefully right now. We aren't sure who your friends or enemies are. Furthermore what would you put in the newspaper as you really don't know the story yet---do you?"

"I'll have to talk to you later," said Josh McDaniel. "There is someone here to see me from the F.B.I. He is showing me his badge. Bring me my typewriter at least and see you later."

"F.B.I.?" responded Rev. Temple as he heard the phone click and silence. Jack began to worry more about his friends as he sat there at his office desk thinking. He wanted to help but it seemed like the only thing to do was pray so he bowed his head and asked God to protect his friends.

"Agent Jennings from the F.B.I. and you must be Josh McDaniel. Is that correct?" the agent asked.

"Yes it is," replied Josh McDaniel. "And what brings you to Sassafras Springs?"

"A matter of major importance," began Agent Jennings. "You must prepare to leave Sassafras Springs immediately."

"I beg your pardon? Why?"

"Your life is in danger just like your parents. You must come with us and let us set up a new identity for you," continued Agent Jennings.

"Change my identity?" said Josh McDaniel with his mouth hanging open in shock. "You think you are going to take me some place and give me a new name? You have to be kidding. What in the world for? What is going on here?"

"Your grandparents Mr. and Mrs. Ronald Coleman were witnesses to the National Bank of St. Louis robbery in 1978. The robbers made off with 12 million dollars. The only ones who were able to identify the robbers were your grandparents. The F.B.I. transferred your grandparents from Arnold, Missouri, to another community and gave them a new name. We thought at the time they would be able to return to their normal lives within the year but the matter got very complicated."

"What do you mean it got complicated?" asked Josh McDaniel.

The agent opened his brief case and pulled out a large file. Josh could see a number of newspaper clippings included with typed pages. The agent placed it in front of him and began pulling out papers and handing to Josh.

"This shows the information about the robbery. It is believed that the Padilla and Kupetis families were the ones who arranged the purchase of the building next door to the bank. From there they tunneled into the bank and were able to blast their way into the back of the safe during the night. Your grandparents had been considering purchasing the same building and had come by at midnight for one more look before making their decision. There they walked in on the operation being carried out. They quickly got behind some large crates and kept quiet. Fortunately for them the robbers were too excited about the amount of money they were carrying and were not paying attention to the entryway."

"My grandparents?" said Josh rather impressed that his grandparents would be preparing to purchase a building downtown and amazed that they managed to observe the robbery without getting killed. "This is a lot for me to digest. Do you have proof of any of this?"

The agent continued sharing information. He started by listing those in the family who had been killed. There was Jasper McDaniel in the car bombing in 1978; Leonard Downwright, Sr. being pushed off the sixth story of the Union Headquarters in 1978; Mr. & Mrs. Winston Downwright being run off the side of the road in the mountains in Colorado in 1979; Melissa (Coleman) McDaniel being killed by poison in 1979 instead of the heart failure reported; Jackson Coleman being killed in prison in 1981; Rachel (Binder) McDaniel killed in the hotel gas explosion in 1985; Lee Downwright, Jr. being hit by a car in Las Vegas; and Jacob Mayfield being killed in Iraq while working as a contractor.

"Wait!" interrupted Josh McDaniel. "You said my

mother was killed by poison? I always questioned her dying of heart disease or failure. Our family has strong hearts. I believed it was from grief. But now you tell me she was poisoned?"

"Yes, and perhaps I should tell you something else," paused Agent Jennings.

"What?" grieved Josh as he thought about his mother and the fact his father had died in a car explosion and new bride in a hotel gas explosion. "What else could there be?"

"You must swear not to tell this to anyone," warned the Agent.

Silence filled the room as the two looked at each other. The agent stepped away and looked out the window for a minute. Finally Josh promised not to tell and pledged to do all he could to help with the case of finding the robbers and the killers that took his loved ones.

"Your mother is still alive," began the Agent. "As soon as you were moved to California to be with your father's parents she was moved to a new location and given a different name. We provided her fake background information so she could get employment. She has been the art teacher in southwest Missouri for these many years since the murders."

Josh looked like he would pass out. He was jubilant inside but couldn't believe it. He stood there shaking and holding on to the edge of the bed. He hoped it was true that his mother was alive.

"She has continued to follow your progress and it has been very difficult for her to remain hidden away. She has asked if you could come meet her and we are prepared to provide a meeting. You must remember one thing. If people are in the area you must act like she is a total stranger. This is to protect both of you."

Josh sat down on the bed. He shook his head back and

forth in disbelief and yet wanted to believe. "I don't know what to say….."

There was a knock at the door as Dollie came charging in saying, "Josh! Are you awake?"

She stopped in her stride as she saw the Agent. She looked at Josh and saw him shaking and tears running down his face. The Agent quickly advised Josh to call the number on the agent's business card when he was ready to take a trip to southwest Missouri. The agent nodded to Dollie and made an exit.

"Who was that?" began Dollie Burgess. "He obviously upset you a lot."

"Not exactly," weakly groaned Josh. "He brought good news in the midst of explaining the situation we are all in at this time."

"So what happened?"

"I can't tell you."

Dollie looked at him in surprise. She stepped back a minute and felt a rush of cold air blow over her as the air conditioning came on. It made her fill with disappointment that Josh could not share the information with her. She shrugged her shoulders.

"You can't tell me," she whined as she took a deep breath. "Ok, I am here for you and when you want to share I'll be ready."

She took hold of Josh and helped him to get back in bed. She pulled the covers up around him, offered him a cookie from the container she had brought, and then turned the lights down. She patted Josh's hand and reassured him she was there to support him through anything that came along. She reminded him of the good old days when they made mud pies, sang songs on the back porch and played house---though sometimes it was more cowboy and Indians.

Josh had barely gotten settled and was almost asleep

when he suddenly realized something surprising about the list of dead in his family that the agent had recited. He turned the light on and shouted to Dollie.

"Call Jack and get him here fast. We have work to do!"

Dollie called Rev. Temple and explained how an F.B.I. agent had been there and that Josh had some surprising news though she didn't know what it was. She encouraged Rev. Temple to come quickly as according to Josh there was work to be done.

On the way to the hospital Rev. Temple spotted Barbara Mayfield and quickly pulled up beside her and invited her to join him as he was going to see Josh. She jumped in and announced that Lee had disappeared. She reported that he had not been at the newspaper all day and all attempts to contact him by phone had failed.

When the two got to the hospital Barbara reported Lee had disappeared to Josh who acted surprised and puzzled.

"Barbara," said Josh McDaniel as he tried to get up but fell back on the bed. Both Barbara and Dollie helped him into a chair while Rev. Temple brought chairs into the room for the ladies. They gathered around the blackboard and sat there silently waiting for Josh to speak. They were eager to know what had happened and what had gotten Josh so excited.

After a few moments to gain strength Josh began sharing what the F.B.I. agent had told him. He revealed how his grandparents had been moved to a new location for having been witnesses to a major crime in St. Louis and had been placed under protection with a new name and new life. Josh ran down the list of those killed in the family.

"Did you hear who was killed?" asked Josh.

"Yes," responded Dollie. "That was awful and that pretty well verifies they all died at the hands of the mob---and that we are all in danger now."

"You missed it," laughed Josh. "So did I the first time. Think about who was on the list."

They went down the list again and then Barbara said, "Wait a minute! Lee Downright, Jr. should not be on the list if Lee Downs is Lee Downwright, Jr. He isn't dead."

"Exactly!" shouted Josh. "So who is Lee Downs?"

"Oh my," worried Dollie. "Now I'm getting scared."

"So who is that serving as an intern?" asked Barbara Mayfield.

"That is what I want to know," replied Josh McDaniel.

"Tell you what I will do," began Rev. Temple. "I will get on Intellius, that business that runs checks on people, and let's see what comes up. I'll be right back."

"What can we do?" asked the two women.

"Barbara, you keep looking for Lee, but be extra careful. We don't have any idea what he will do now. He could be dangerous."

"You have that right!" laughed Barbara Mayfield. "I need to drive to Warrensville to get some groceries for the weekend. I believe I saw in the ledger that Lee had paid for a room at the Colonial Western Motel last week when he disappeared and then showed up with a complete newspaper. I bet he has a place over there to work to prevent us from knowing exactly what he is doing. I'll make the trip count for two things. I'll be back in about 40 minutes."

"You could be right," agreed Josh McDaniel. "I bet he has the wildest newspaper ever, but we are going to have one too. We'll out fox that guy."

"Now Josh," interrupted Dollie, "make sure you don't get like him."

"No, Dollie," laughed Josh. "We will print facts and back up everything with evidence. That is the way a newspaper should be. We must be the watch dog of society and you can't do that if you have an agenda or aim to make a lot of money on sensationalism. People count on us to tell the truth."

Rev. Temple returned shortly to report that he could not find anything on Lee Downs or Lee Downwright, Jr. or anything related. Barbara returned with news that Lee was in fact staying at the Colonial Western Motel in Warrensville. She said she could hear typing on the computer outside his room. They all agreed it was probably the newspaper for the next day which made it even more important to prepare another newspaper to distribute to reveal the facts that Lee would be ignoring.

In two hours the entire group was busily preparing a newspaper. Headlines on the layout sheets revealed that a local family was in the witness protection program as they waited to testify against a major crime group. Another story reported that the Mayor had been exonerated for accusations of a drunken and abusive lifestyle by a local reporter as facts had proven otherwise. An apology was issued to the Missouri State Attorney General for being forced to leave during demonstrations caused by false reports printed in the newspaper. Apologies also appeared for all the other people who had been insulted and used by Lee Downs as subjects for his sensationalized headlines and news items over the past few weeks.

The regular printing staff entered the print shop of the newspaper quietly hoping to not find Lee Downs. They were relieved to begin printing and to complete work without a disturbance. The newspaper was printed and bundled and ready. They loaded the newspapers in the van and drove away with them to keep them securely safe until needed.

CHAPTER FIFTEEN

The next day Dollie ran excitedly into Josh McDaniel's room. Catching her breath she shook Josh gently to wake him up. He rolled over and looked curiously at her.

"Yes," he began, "and what has gotten you so excited today?"

"The mayor is having a press conference at ten a.m. The F.B.I. will be there as well," she reported.

"Well, now," paused Josh rubbing his chin. "Wonder what they are going to do?"

"I don't know but they have sent word for you to be there if at all possible."

Josh blinked his eyes and said, "You mean I could leave the hospital? Let's get a move on and go!"

They both laughed as the doctor entered the room. Dr. Boling looked at their merriment and expressed that maybe the work had been good for Josh even though it was against the doctor's better judgment. The doctor agreed Josh seemed stronger and obviously was in good spirits.

"So, I'm well enough to go to the mayor's press conference at 10 a.m.?" asked Josh McDaniel.

"The what?" coughed the Doctor. "I don't believe anyone

said anything about you going anywhere. We have you lined up for surgery on Wednesday. Did you forget that?"

"No," sighed Josh McDaniel, "but this is very important."

"Everything is important to you, Josh," laughed Dr. Boling. "I trust that our faithful and dedicated Dollie will remain with you while you are gone to the press conference?"

"Absolutely, Sir," answered Dollie as the doctor nodded to her.

"You know how important it is to keep him quiet," asked Dr. Boling.

"Yes, Sir," agreed Dollie.

"If you don't mind I think we'll take you in the ambulance and bring you right back. The fact is, the F.B.I. did ask and made arrangements for you to be there. I didn't have much say in the matter, but I think you can handle it. Please do try to be quiet though. Don't get excited and certainly don't stand up and start walking around. We'll wheel you in using a wheelchair and wheel you back. Got it?"

"We've got it and I pledge to behave," promised Josh McDaniel.

The doctor exited as the phone rang next to Josh's bed. Dollie answered it and sounded surprised. She looked at Josh and then gave out a laugh. She turned away and continued to talk.

Rev. Temple entered the room with a stack of newspapers and handed one to Josh.

"Here they are. Yours and Lee's."

"Do I dare look?"

"I think you will be very surprised," said Rev. Temple with a smile on his face.

Josh took the newspaper and read it cover to cover.

Every type of groan could be heard coming from him as he made his way through the newspaper. There on the front page were the photographs from the album that Lee had brought to the hospital to share with Josh. An explanation of who was in each picture and how everyone was related was all presented for the world to see. The witness protection effort was now destroyed and the F.B.I. would have to decide what to do.

"Order, order," said Mayor Wallingford as he pounded his gavel in the city hall conference room as the meeting began. "I have called a press conference today to announce my resignation. My wife and I have chosen to withdraw from public life for the next few years while we enjoy our daughter, Barbara, and renew our family connections. The past three decades have been very stressful for my wife as she sought to keep her true identity from everyone including me. I had no idea she was Jackson Coleman's sister."

Photographers started snapping pictures and reporters shot hands in the air to ask questions at this announcement.

"Please, hold your questions as there is a lot to share with you today," said Mayor Wallingford as he tried to calm the audience. "I promise to answer questions at the end once all the information has been provided to you."

There on the front row was Lee Downs with camera in hand, tape recorder hanging from his neck recording everything being said and a notepad on his lap.

"Excuse me Mayor Wallingford!" interrupted Lee Downs. "Jackson Coleman---isn't that the man you railroaded into jail where he was killed for embezzlement---a crime you committed?" Lee Downs shouted.

"Lee, my little nephew, let's talk about that," began

Mayor Wallingford. The crowd gasped as Mayor Wallingford focused completely on the reporter.

"Did he just call the reporter his nephew?" a reporter shouted.

"You killed Lee Downwright, my father!" accused Lee Downs.

"No," said Mayor Wallingford quietly and in complete control. "Lee, your father was a friend of mine. He introduced my wife and me at a party in his house. Your father isn't Lee Downwright, but rather Jackson Coleman. You know your name isn't Lee Downs but rather Roger Coleman. I had not seen you in many years and had nearly forgotten that Randall Coleman had a son. When Randall was here to speak the other day he spotted you at the demonstration. Yes, ladies and gentlemen, this is Roger Coleman, son of State Attorney General Randall Coleman. Randy reported to me that Roger has become a problem the past couple of years since getting into a pro-terrorist organization at the university. According to Attorney Coleman, Roger is determined to make me pay for his grandfather's death under the guise that he was Lee Downwright's son. Unknown to Roger is the fact that Lee is his first cousin."

Dollie leaned over Josh's shoulder and said, "Well, I didn't see that one coming. Good for the Mayor."

"We are in fact having a rather remarkable and unusual family reunion today," said Mayor Wallingford as he turned back to the rostrum and began again. Lee Downs/Roger Coleman stood up to leave.

"Where are you going?" said Deputy Harris as he placed his hand on Lee Downs/Roger Coleman's shoulder and pressed him back into his chair. "You have an excellent spot to watch the rest of the presentation. In fact I think I'll stay here with you."

"No need," said Roger Coleman alias Lee Downs as he

tried to get away. "I can do without all this family reunion stuff."

"I suspect you will be pleasantly surprised if you stay," replied Officer Harris.

The Mayor directed the people to look at the newspapers being handed out and to compare the newspapers. He noted which was prepared by Lee/Roger and which by Josh.

"As you can see a number of people in town are related that perhaps you didn't know were related. Many of us, including myself, are just becoming aware of this. It took some doing to sort through everything but I think we have an accurate story to share with you today. My wife is Mollie Coleman. Her last name was changed to Collins when her parents had to go into the witness protection program. They were originally Mr. & Mrs. Ronald Coleman, but the F. B. I gave them the new names of Mr. & Mrs. Riley Collins in 1978. Some of you will remember the Collins as being very helpful neighbors."

Several in the audience nodded approval that the Collins had been good people. A brief applause was sounded as the people remembered the fine couple.

Mayor Wallingford continued, "The couple was relocated by the F.B.I. after they had been witnesses to the robbery at the National Bank of St. Louis of 12 million dollars in 1978. Mr. and Mrs. Ronald Coleman alias Mr. & Mrs. Riley Collins were the only ones that could identify the robbers. Because of this their lives were immediately in danger with the mob putting contracts out for them to be killed. It is now proven that the well known mobster families, the Padilla and Kupetis families, were the ones who arranged the purchase of the building next door to the bank. From there they tunneled into the bank and were able to blast their way into the back of the safe during the night. Mr. & Mrs. Coleman alias Collins were considering purchasing the building and entered the building at midnight when they saw a light on. They wanted to take one last look before calling the realtor to make a deal. They were lucky they were able to hide behind some crates and were not found by the Gang."

Photographers were snapping pictures again and reporters were frantically waving hands. Mayor Wallingford motioned for them to remain silent and continued with the presentation.

"Mr. & Mrs. Collins were mysteriously killed in a car accident in 1978. Another daughter, Melissa, sister to my wife, had married Jasper McDaniel who moved to Sassafras Springs. The F. B. I. had not changed her name thinking she would not be connected to the newly named Collins. Unfortunately they were wrong as the mob killed Jasper with a car bomb and is believed to have poisoned Melissa in 1978. Jasper and Melissa were the parents of our newspaper editor Josh McDaniel."

Applause followed the mention of Josh McDaniel and some stood to show respect and appreciation for the man. They were glad to see him able to be present at the meeting. Dollie patted him on the back.

Mayor Wallingford continued, "Josh was told that his mother died of heart failure and there was a funeral but I'm pleased to announce tonight that she is here with us. The F.B.I. changed her name and moved her to a new location and here she is Josh. Your mother is here to give you a hug she has wanted to give you for the past 3 decades."

Josh, wide eyed and beaming was stunned to see his beautiful mother come from a side room. She ran to him and they began to cry. Despite Dollie's effort to keep Josh in the wheelchair, he lifted himself from the chair and welcomed his mother with a big hug. The mayor motioned for the audience to return to silence after they applauded and started whispering to each other.

"Another daughter of the Ronald Coleman's," began Mayor Wallingford, "was Millie Coleman. She married Winston Downwright. Here again the name was not changed and I now know that Leonard Downwright that worked for me in Arnold was her son. Because the name was not changed it is believed that Leonard was pushed off a sixth story of the Union Headquarters killing him instantly. His wife was immediately given a new identity and moved to a new location. The grandson, Lee, was taken care of by his grandparents, Millie and Winston after the son's death. The baby was with them when they were run off a mountain road. The baby miraculously was thrown clear of the inferno that devoured the trailer and car when it hit the ground at the base of the mountain. Tonight it is wonderful to be able to welcome home my grand nephew, Lee Downwright, and his mother, Jacklyn Downwright, both of whom were given new identities and have been living in a different area the past three decades."

Mrs. Wallingford got up from her chair and approached Jacklyn and Lee as they entered the room. Melissa also left Josh and went to meet her relatives. The four lined up in front of the Mayor with Josh being rolled up in the wheelchair by Barbara Mayfield as the family was reunited.

Mayor Wallingford continued, "We have lost many members of our family. Starting with Mr. & Mrs. Ronald Coleman alias Riley Collins in 1978; Jasper McDaniel in 1978; Leonard Downwright, Sr. in 1978; Mr. & Mrs. Winston Downwright in 1979; Rachel Binder McDaniel in a gas explosion at a hotel that Josh was to be inside in Los Angeles in 1985; and Jacob Mayfield, husband of my daughter, killed in Iraq while working as a contractor. All of these have been proven to be murders."

The crowd murmured among themselves as they looked the information over in the newspapers and the notes they had taken. Finally a few people stood and started applauding. The Mayor and his family bowed their heads in appreciation and took a seat on the platform. Next F.B.I. Agent Brasel took a position at the microphone.

Mayor Wallingford continued, "We were led to believe that Melissa, Lee Downwright, Jr., and Jackson Coleman were all killed too. We are pleased to introduce Jackson to you to make our family complete."

"Grandpa!" yelled Roger Coleman alias Lee Downs. "Grandpa is a live?"

Officer Harris released the young man and allowed him to go to his grandfather Jackson Coleman as he came from the side room.

"Ladies and Gentlemen, my name is Ray Brasel and I am an agent with the F.B.I. There are some other things that need to be added to the information already presented. These people who were killed would probably have never been killed had it not been for a zealous newspaper reporter back in 1978 who printed information about a birthday party that the McDaniels, Wallingfords, Colemans and Downwrights all attended. The newspaper alerted the Padilla and Kupetis Gang of where the various family members were located. Despite an effort to get the reporter not to print the item it appeared in the newspaper and three months later six people were dead. Others were to follow."

The crowd stared at Agent Brasel with eyes filling with tears and mouths open. There was not a sound in the room. They listened for the next announcement in this expanding mystery.

"We are happy to report that arrests were issued last night for 21 individuals in the Padilla and Kupetis Gang. We are confident that thanks to this family the Gang will be put behind bars for a very long time. The evidence is concrete for all of the murders. This family should be able to return to normal lives today. Our thanks is extended to them for their determination to stand for what is right and good."

The crowd stood and applauded. Even Roger Coleman alias Lee Downs was smiling and hugging all the family members. Josh shook the young man's hand as Roger apologized for ruining the newspaper. Roger admitted that he had made a huge mistake by working to sell the newspapers with partial truths and sensationalizing.

Agent Brasel continued, "There is one more thing to share with you. It was found that Jackson Coleman did not embezzle the money at the Union. All charges have been dropped. It was not Mayor Wallingford or Leonard Downwright. The entire thing was a hoax set forth by the Padilla and Kupetis Gang to cause the Coleman family trouble putting pressure on Mr. & Mrs. Ronald Coleman so they would not testify concerning the bank robbery."

The crowd cheered and applauded again.

Agent Brasel continued, "One mystery remains. There is still the matter of the missing money. Somewhere out there is one million dollars which is all that is left to find of the twelve million stolen. If anyone can help us we would greatly appreciate it. Now are there any questions?"

CHAPTER SIXTEEN

After the completion of the press conference, the entire family went to the Wallingford's house to celebrate. Even Roger/alias Lee was invited and was joined by his father, State Attorney General Randall Coleman. Randall was quite surprised and excited to find his father Jackson Coleman was still living and exonerated from the crime for which he had been sent to jail. It was quite a reunion.

During the festivities Roger excused himself and went to his apartment to get his grandfather's trunk. He was sure the family would enjoy seeing the items inside the trunk. He was not wrong. They were very excited when they heard he was bringing it to the Wallingford's. Most figured the trunk had been sold or lost. Most everyone had memories of keeping their toys and other things in the trunk and were eager to see it again.

Leonard Downwright, Jr. and Roger became instant friends as remarkably both had become journalists. They laughed at how the real Lee had become editor of the Mountain Home Journal having graduated from the University of Missouri in Columbia a couple of years earlier.

The family marveled how there were three journalists in the same family with Josh, Lee and Roger. Barbara announced there would soon be four as she was entering the university to major in journalism. She reported that she had never had so much fun trying to break the mystery of the family with Josh McDaniel.

Roger and Lee carried the heavy trunk into the Wallingford's house. Everyone gathered around it and listened to Mrs. Wallingford and Jackson Coleman share the history of the trunk. Then they handed each item to the family members as they told where each item came from and why it was in the trunk. It was a very special time for the family.

Roger was glad he shared his great-grandparents things with the family and more importantly was excited about having a family again. His life had been a very strange and unpredictable one since his grandfather had entered prison. Suddenly it seemed like all the puzzles were solved and all the questions were answered.

The family was fascinated with the letters and photographs. Inside the trunk were coloring books, checkers, dominoes and some jacks. There were grade cards for all the children and a few pieces of clothing that the triplets and Randall wore as babies.

Josh didn't return to the hospital right away and Dollie stayed with him to keep him from over doing it. Dollie and the doctor understood how important it was for him to be at the family get together. Josh rolled his wheelchair beside the trunk and smiled. He remembered the old trunk as one of his favorite things to play in when visiting his grandparents at a very young age. He had even hidden in it one time.

He asked the people to stand back and knocked on the side releasing a lever that threw open the bottom of the box. He bent over with help from Dollie. The family heard the click and suddenly they were all leaning over to see in the box. There in the bottom of the trunk was something that sparkled.

"My word!" exclaimed the entire family.

"That's gold!" shouted Roger. "No wonder the trunk was so heavy. I can't believe it. All these years I've been carrying around a fortune. Hahaha!"

Josh promptly called the F.B.I. and turned the million dollars in gold over to them while the family questioned how the bars got in the bottom of the old trunk. The family couldn't help but wonder if great-grandfather Ronald Coleman had helped himself when in that bank, but that will be another mystery for another time and definitely not headline news for the Colemans.

AUTHOR'S BIOGRAPHY
BOB WYATT

Robert W. "Bob" Wyatt was born in Johnson County and reared in the small town of Leeton, Missouri. Graduating from the local high school he continued his education with a B.S. in Bible from Central Christian College of the Bible in Moberly, MO; a Bachelor of Music Education and M.S. in Education from the University of Central Missouri, Warrensburg; and correspondence work from Johnson Bible College, Kimberlin Heights, Tennessee.

He has had over 40 books published dealing with family and local histories and was the driving force in establishing the Leeton Museum. Other work experience included ministering to two congregations; heading The Christian Government Ministry which provided spiritual encouragement to the Missouri legislature; editor/owner of three small town newspapers and a two county shopper; restoration of an 1835 house and converting it into a restaurant; high school band and choir director; and is currently involved in setting up drama productions both in Missouri and Europe in a cultural exchange he organized between his hometown and Leicester, England six years ago.

He currently serves on the Leeton City Council and is president of the Mineral Creek Historical Society. In his spare time he volunteers as curator for the local museum. He has served as a deacon, teacher, superintendent of the Sunday school and worked in many positions in church camps and vacation Bible Schools. His love for life is demonstrated in his effort to serve others emphasizing the need for people to work together to lift each other to higher levels of accomplishment and Christian witness.

BOOK SUMMARY

"The Watch Dog Is Mad" (third book of the Bachelor Preacher's Mystery Series) features the editor of the Sassafras Springs Gazette and his intern. The editor has a heart attack and while in the hospital watches his intern turn the town upside down with sensationalized stories. The bachelor preacher assists the editor in teaching the town, the intern and a family the intern didn't know he had that telling the truth is important.